JON DOUST

TO THE HIGHLANDS

JON DOUST

TO THE HIGHLANDS

FREMANTLE PRESS
fine independent publishing

For M and M

From Dr Ian Palmer, MD
27 June 1969

Mr Jack Muir initially presented with many ailments including a recurring knee injury, deafness in one ear and what he referred to as a 'kind of STD'. Painkillers and physiotherapy solved the first ailment, followed by a prompt ENT referral to investigate a probable cause for his deafness. Mr Muir's 'STD' was in fact an NSU (non-specific urethritis), a term covering a plethora of unknown causes for sexually transmitted urethritis. Most troubling were Mr Muir's psychological issues resultant from delayed stress regarding episodes he wished to remain confidential. Naturally he was referred immediately to Dr Grey Hammond, a highly respected psychiatrist, specialising in cases of what is referred to as stress response syndrome.

From Dr Grey Hammond, FRCPsych, FRANZCP
3 October 1973

Mr Jack Muir is well known to this practitioner and one considers him a highly moral person. Like many men he spent much of his youth sowing oats that grew into thistles. As part of his ongoing therapy one encouraged him to keep a journal of his thoughts, feelings and memories. That journal grew into this book. Professional ethics prevent one from disclosing any specific matters discussed between counsellor and client.

What one can add is that there have been many sociological studies undertaken in the region where Mr Muir 'spent time' and it is not unreasonable to suggest that much of his sexual behaviour, for which he has punished himself severely, would not have been out of the ordinary among local populations regardless of their racial origins.

PART ONE

1

The man on me moves.

I lie still.

He moves again. Maybe he's embarrassed to be murdering a sobbing, bleeding, blubbering man who has no power, no strength, no will, no future. He rolls off me. I squeeze my eyes. Lungs suck great chunks of air. I hear him stand and walk away. I don't know where to but I hope it's far, so far I can't see him when I get up off this floor because then I might stumble down the stairs to the kitchen, take one of the houseboy's long knives, walk up the stairs to his room, open his door, find him lying on his bed exhausted from the attempted murdering and stick him – stick the knife into his musclebound body more than once, maybe as many times as the murder I heard about on Radio Australia last week when one man stabbed another to death because of a sweet potato deal gone sour.

I turn my head to the floor. The crying spreads. I am emptying, pouring out, everything is leaving me. I know that if I cry long enough and hard enough there will be nothing left but a wet patch of tears mixed with blood, and when he comes out of his room to check on me, or someone climbs the stairs, all they will see is a small pool of what was once me.

2

When I stepped off the plane in the capital, I stepped into a stinking, rotting, decaying, forever composting wet heat, and right into the care of two seasoned bank johnnies who drove me direct to a tropical pub full of cane furniture. They didn't take me to the bank to meet the manager, the assistant manager, the accountant, or up the hill to meet the district commissioner. They said all that could wait.

First things first, said Tony, who was leaving at the end of the week for Sydney and his old job at head office. For us expatriates, the islands are all about drinking and fucking. One is easy to come by and the other depends on your preferences.

I smiled, sat back in the big cane chair and looked around me. Tony and the other bloke, whose name I didn't get and I don't think I ever saw him again, were wearing the standard white shirt, white shorts and long white socks. A great start, straight to the pub, no looking around for cops hunting underage drinkers, or adults who might know how old I was and tell me I was too young to drink. When it was my buy I didn't even have to walk up to the bar because a solid black man in a skirt walked up to our table and asked if we wanted more drinks. I said yes and he went away to get them.

I might get used to this, I said.

You've only got two years, Jack, said Tony, and if you get used to it, by then it's time to leave. As for me, it's been fun but I can't wait to get home and see a bit more white flesh.

Most people in the lounge bar were white. All the waiters were black. As I looked around I noticed I was the only one looking around. Then I saw her, the mixed race woman. Tony looked at me.

Yes, he said, she's stunning, but not for you, or any of us.

Why not?

Not because of her colour, mate, because she's taken, by some bloody shipping millionaire.

She was magnificent, all the way down from her face, through her neck, shoulders, arms, breasts, stomach, thighs and legs and in that way she moved, sat and placed one leg so carefully over its equal and opposite. I almost died there and then but couldn't because she became a dream and I decided I wouldn't wake up until she, or someone just like her, was lying beside me with a perfect leg draped over one of mine.

The other bloke said, Trouble, Jack, you're looking at trouble.

How would you know? said Tony. Not only has your wife got her hooks in your pants, you've never left the capital.

I just know. Look what happened to Dixy.

What happened to Dixy? I asked.

No one really knows, said Tony.

He went completely bloody troppo, said the other bloke.

Yeah, but we don't know why. Plenty of rumours about him and a native woman. Anyway, he was coming to work dishevelled and drunk, lost the plot and had to go home early.

My grandfather always said: The best breeds are always pure. You don't breed a mongrel with a thoroughbred. You don't put a purebred Friesian in with a Jersey, or an Arab with a Clydesdale. But from where I was sitting I decided he didn't have a clue what he was talking about and later, while lying on top of a bed they gave me in the old archive room, I dreamt of my own paddock full of mixed breeds walking around looking at me with their eyes full of mischief and intent.

I slept on top of the bed because of the heat but they didn't really put me in an old archive room. I was given a bed in a room in the old men's quarters but there was no fan in the ceiling and the heavy, dripping heat forced me into the archive room where I shoved my bed right under the huge propeller that not only kept me awake most of the night with its screaming whirling, it also kept me dry and blew the mosquitoes out of the building and caused me to pull on a sheet and a thin blanket.

The next morning I woke with a hangover in a room full of documents. At first I thought I was dreaming and had gone to hell which wasn't full of fire and burning sinners but paper and more paper and I'd better get started or the fires would begin. The fan soon blew away the cobwebs and I managed to find my way to the showers. I washed, dried and returned to my designated room, the one without the documents, and opened the wardrobe.

Jesus Christ, I yelled.

Cockroaches, thousands of them, scurried away from open spaces. I grabbed a pair of underpants and more dropped on the floor. I shook them and even more fell. Great. What a town. No room in the new, modern bank mess up the road and my clothes were home to seething millions of the creature most feared and despised by neat, tidy and clean people like Rotarians. The other thing I did that first morning was take double my dose of malaria pills.

3

It was 1968. The world was falling apart. Bits of it were burning. In Europe, Britain and America students were running amok. In Perth they did what they always did: studied, got pissed, stumbled in and out of relationships, played tennis, went to the beach, fought, fucked, bragged about fucks that never existed, and drove cars into fences, trees and other cars. When I left school most of the kids in my year went on to university, as they should, because my old school, Grammar School for Boys, expected it, their parents expected it, they expected it. They were future leaders and had to be groomed to take over. My shocked parents did not cope well with my final exam results and my mother tried to rip my face off. Dad stepped in, pushed Mum out of the way, and gave me to the bank, Australia's first bank, The Colonial Bank of Australia. He grabbed me by the scruff of the neck and hauled me down to the local branch and said to the manager: Take him, or I'll kill him. Well, he didn't say that, but his look did.

I hated the bank. My career was a series of fits and starts. I was good with people, so my enquiry counter work was well reviewed. Numbers were not a strong point and so my stints as a batch clerk, agency teller relief and ledger examiner with responsibility for balancing the day's incomings and outgoings across the entire branch, were not well reported. My weeks were long, boring and highlighted by the daily early-morning erection. Once I was on the bus and it began its stop–start routine there was nothing I could do to stem the rising lizard. I enjoyed the sensation, and hated the embarrassment.

I wasn't alone; there were other bankers like me, failed sons on early-morning buses, battling bulging pants and wealthy middle-class parents who had spent thousands on exclusive, wasted educations. We were biding our time, waiting for an opportunity to crop up, dad to give us a job in the family business, grandfather to die and leave us a million, a mate to score us a job with his stockbroker father, or another one to fix us up with an easy job making big money with his dad's mining company, or marriage to that blonde chick, the one whose parents owned the supermarket chain.

Some mornings I woke, full of the heavy clouds from the night before, and sat there, on the end of the bed, wondering what sort of a life it was, the one I was living. I had a job I detested, worked with people who bored the shit out of me, like the accountant in the Gosnells branch who insisted on talking to me about farm machinery because he grew up on a farm and he once met my dad and I couldn't say anything like you're a knob, mate, and you're giving me the shits because if I did he might give me a bad report and I'd be back working the batch clerk's job which was the most boring job in the entire banking system because all you did all day was pick up forms, stamp them, sort them and hand them over to the ledger examiner who was the next most boring person in the branch and all he wanted to talk about was English soccer because that's where he was from and when he did he talked with one of those whingeing accents that turned your blood cold and your fists hot.

Dad wanted me to sit my leaving and matriculation exams again. He made me go to night-school. I hardly ever went because I knew I'd only fail again and because the two TAFE teachers looked like they belonged in a bank. Whenever I spoke to Dad or Mum on the phone, or they visited the city, all I ever got was: Why can't you be more like your brother Thomas? Or Tim Bentley, who was studying medicine, or Barbara Perkins, who was studying history? Even most of the boys in my class, the bottom class, got into university. Thomas was in university studying law. I was working in a bank. Down at the Rotary club the conversation was all about Thomas.

Someone in the back of my head kept talking to me. It might have been Jesus or the Phantom, I could never put a name to him, but he kept on at me about living a good and moral life and doing unto others as I would have done unto me and fighting injustice and defeating the communist bastards, but the voice wasn't strong enough and I found myself living the strange life of someone I didn't know, someone I had happened upon while in search of the real me.

.....

The day I flew out to the islands, Dad had a Rotary conference to attend in Bunbury. He had to be there, not only because he was president of the Genoralup club but because he was working his way through the ranks of other club presidents and aiming to become a district governor. I drove down to see them the weekend before. As usual we sat around the kitchen table, drinking Mum's all-milk coffee brew and taking conversation leads from Dad.

I still don't think it's a good idea, said Dad. But when you come home I'd like you to give a talk at Rotary.

Sure, I said.

And remember to eat plenty of salt and take your malaria pills.

Right.

That was pretty much it. Mum cried, of course, kissed me with her lips pursed and Dad crushed my hand. Dad didn't say what he really thought and neither did I. Why would we? What good would it do? He thought I was useless and didn't believe for a minute that the bank had chosen me, that I was a chosen one, that it was grooming me for higher office. And I thought he was a prick who was determined to make sure my life was as dull and lacking in adventure as his and his Rotarian mates'. We were Grammar School boys, all of us: Dad, my older brother Thomas, and everybody who meant anything to anybody including young brother Bill who was already booked in for his high school years.

．．．．．

My old schoolmate, Brett Jones, picked me up and took me to Perth airport. There was a mob there to see me off. Some old school friends, a few mates from the bank, a couple of blokes from the football club and an almost, could have been, girlfriend, Megan Stirling. She was going out with a friend of mine but as soon as she saw me she would laugh. Older blokes told me that was a good sign, if a girl laughed at you, or with you, I wasn't sure which was best, or what the difference was. They said I should have a crack at her, make a move, step in, work my charm. I wasn't sure. Her boyfriend was a mate. But Megan arrived at the airport alone.

Megan had great hair. You could see she worked on her hair. She was about my height and when she walked her eyes sort of danced around and her hips kind of swayed and her legs formed calves. I loved a leg with a calf. When I was in high school I was desperately in love with the well-calved Sandra Johnston who was interschool one hundred yards champion and I wanted her calves and mine to lock and rub because I was fast too and my calves were strong and well defined but I wasn't a champion, only ever good enough for the relay team.

Megan liked me. I could tell by the way her eyes found mine and the way her mouth almost laughed as soon as I spoke her name: Megan Stirling, oh yes, stirling.

Everyone was pretty happy. The Orbit Inn at Perth airport seemed to have different rules to the rest of the city. The beers flowed over the bar and no one said: Hey you! You're underage. In West Australia the drinking age was twenty-one and I couldn't wait to get to the islands because there the drinking age was the same as in Victoria and New South Wales, eighteen. If the drinking age was eighteen, I reckoned it probably meant a lot of other things were possible too, like the things you'd heard about Sydney, Sin City, and other things, things I hadn't thought of, things I had thought of but was too shy or afraid to mention, and things that were impossible anywhere else on earth.

As all the blokes pushed me towards the departure gate, stumbling and dropping my carry-on luggage, Megan came up behind me and put her arms around me. I turned my face into her face and we kissed, full on. The blokes yelled and whistled but we kept on kissing and I could feel my pants tighten due to the lizard growing inside them. When she let my lips go she whispered in my ear: We should have done that ages ago. My face got hot and red and I pretended to stumble again and the sound of her laughter only encouraged the lizard and so I ran away to the gate that led to the plane that led to Sydney where I caught the next plane that led to the islands.

4

Hey, yelled a man at my door.

Jesus! You scared the shit out of me.

Yeah, he said, you me too. Gidday, I'm Ted Robinson.
From Brisbane.

What are you doing here?

I live in a room down the back. You must be the new
bloke from Perth.

Must be. Jack Muir.

We shook hands. Ted was one of those blokes you liked,
soon as you set eyes on him. Tall, rangy, tanned, broad-
shouldered, just what you'd imagine a Queenslander
would look like.

Breakfast?

Huh? Yeah. Where?

Up the new mess. Didn't anyone tell you anything?
I've got a motorbike. I'll give you a lift.

You think I should put my pants on?

Ha ha. Might as well. The sheilas up there aren't worth
leaving them off for.

Robinson rode a motorbike like you would imagine a
Queenslander would, hell for leather, low around a bend,
fast as Flint up a hill, zippy across an intersection, all the
while talking his head off over his shoulder.

There's a good bunch of blokes in the bank, he yelled.
Most nights we go to a bar over in the satellite town,
Bulimbi. Some of the sheilas go too but they aren't much
to look at. A big night is when a mob of mixed race tarts
turn up. Oh, mate, they are something.

As he talked I kept my eyes on the road. It wasn't
much of a road but I grew up in a house at the end of a
gravel track, so anything with bitumen was okay by me.
This road was sealed but it looked like great lumps of tar
had been tossed off the back of a truck. Along the road

natives walked, mostly men and some women with things sitting on or hanging off their heads. The vegetation looked sparse and dry, not the lush tropical growth I had expected.

Looks a bit dry, I yelled at the back of Robinson's head.

Won't be long, he yelled back. The wet season'll get underway any minute.

When Robinson turned his bike off in the new bank mess driveway, he stood beside his Honda Black Bomber and said: What do you reckon?

Nice bike, I said.

I love it and there's one more thing I gotta have before I leave this bloody place.

What's that?

A trip to the Islands of Love.

What?

You never heard of them?

Nuh.

They're on the other side of the main island. I know blokes who've been there. They reckon you just walk up to sheilas, ask for a fuck and if they like the look of you, you're in. Sex is just a game for them.

You're joking.

Nuh. You interested?

Of course I was, but I didn't say it out loud. I wanted sex, I was clear about that, but I was still a virgin, and still a bit scared of the wrath of a God who was no longer with me, or didn't exist. Then there was the wrath of a mother who believed that sex was created by the Heavenly Man so we could reproduce, and fucking for fun was a sin and deserving of retribution.

The dining room was nothing like my old boarding school dining room. It was like a large restaurant with modern chairs, tables, no prefects at their heads, all very civilised. People lined up for food served by native men

18

through a servery. The furniture and general decor was plain and functional but the view out the large windows and across the bay was spectacular.

Come on, Jacky, let's get food, said Robinson. After breakfast I'll take you down to the bank and we'll see if we can't get the day off to ride you around town.

As people passed us they said: Gidday, Robbo. And: What are you up to, Robbo? Then: You already corrupted the new bloke, Robbo? Finally: Jesus, Robbo, haven't they sent you home yet?

. . . .

Right after breakfast, we walked into the main branch of the bank. It sat on the ground floor of the two-storey building, just below the old quarters where Robbo and I lived as the only occupants.

You better come meet the branch accountant, said Robbo. He said he knows you. He's a West Aussie too.

There was no need to find his office, Richard Symons was already out of it and walking towards us. That must have been why I got the job, my big break in the banking world, because Symons had headed the two bank training schools back in Perth, the two schools where Jack Muir shone, rose above the pack. There you are, Jack, said Symons. Good to see you again. How was your flight?

Great, Mr Symons, I said. It was a long flight but I managed to stay above ground.

You still have your sense of humour, Jack. That's good, you'll need it here. And, by the way, we are not as formal in the islands, so, please, call me Richard.

Thanks, Richard, I will.

Ted here has asked that you two have the day off so he can show you around town. Are you happy with that arrangement?

Sure, I'm just not so sure about his bike riding.

No one is, said Symons. But look, let's make it half a day off, because I want you to come back here to see what we have in store for you. Given your knowledge and intelligence, we have quite a challenge for you and I believe you are up to it.

Gee, thanks, Richard. Okay.

Robbo lifted his eyebrows at me as we walked out the main entrance, past two neatly dressed white girls. I almost missed them because I was going over Symons' words.

Deep inside me there was a small part making noises, maybe wanting to believe in me and hoping to show the disbelievers back home that I had something, could do something, if I wanted to, if I felt like it. The old headmaster. Dad. Mum. My brothers. It would be a new experience, to make good; I'd have to stay focussed, to concentrate, to dedicate, to strive for consistency. I felt nervous, anxious, but ready. I decided to buy some salt to keep in my room because salt would help me keep my cool. When I was a kid I was diagnosed with pinks disease, mercury poisoning, and the family doctor reckoned salt would help me stay calm. I wasn't sure, I still experienced sudden rushes of anxiety, but I loved salt and most days ate a handful of the stuff. And when drinking I couldn't keep my hands off the beer nuts and the potato chips.

I laughed out loud.

What? said Robbo.

Symons, I said. Did you hear what he said about me?

Yeah, he's got the hots for you.

Ha ha. You got any idea what he has in mind?

Nuh, but I'd keep your pants on at night and maybe rig up a piece of string and some tin cans, so if he comes into your room you'll hear him before he gets to your bed.

Shut up you filthy bastard. Get on your bike. Let's go see some naked ladies.

The capital looked like a frontier town, a town struggling to find itself in a maze of buildings randomly erected. Robbo rode around it like he owned it, yelling over his head and occasionally whistling at attractive mixed race girls. It might have been 1968 but there was no sign of it here, no hippies and no bearded students marching against colonialism, capitalism, fascism or calling for free love. Not all the white people wore white but they were all neatly dressed and behaving in an orderly manner.

Do you play footy? he yelled.

Which one?

Aerial ping-pong, you wanker. You sandgropers only know how to play one.

It's a better game than chimp footy.

What?

Chimp footy. You play an ape's game.

Robbo took both his hands off the handlebars and made like a chimp, just for a second, but long enough for my guts to hit my throat.

There were no naked ladies in town that day, but Robinson took me up a hill to see the sights from high, then down the hill and across town to the place we would visit often at night in many futile attempts to find the perfect mix of feminine beauty: Melanesian, European and Asian. When I say futile, I don't mean ladies approaching perfection did not visit, they did, but they were usually on the arm of some flash, rich, or important, prick.

5

Robinson turned into the back of the bank, stopped his Honda and said: What do you think so far?

I told you, I said. It's a great bike.

No, you goose, about this place, the capital, the island.

I reckon I'll survive, I said. As long as work doesn't interfere too much.

Yeah, you'll be fine, just don't let them real bank johnnies get their hooks in you, or before you know it you'll be just like them and your life might as well be over.

We were still laughing as we walked in through the main doors. Robinson went off to his desk to do whatever it was he had to do. I had no idea and never found out. I went to Symons' office. It was a big room in the middle of the building. The only windows looked out into the bank itself. Symons stood up and shook my hand again.

It's good to have you here, Jack, he said. I've been trying to lift the calibre of the personnel on staff.

Thank you, Richard, I said. I only hope I'm up to it. You're not going to give me too big a challenge, are you?

What I have in mind is the second teller. It has a cash holding of around fifty thousand dollars, so it's a big responsibility. Have you ever used a pistol?

My mind was racing in a mad fluster of fear and pride and an energy I had not felt before.

No, I haven't, I said. Who do I have to kill?

Symons looked like he was about to laugh, almost laughed, held back, then allowed a small shift in one corner of his mouth.

Seriously, Jack, we'll have to send you out to the firing range for a bit of practice. As you know it is a standard regulation that all tellers must have firearms training.

I almost said, look, Symons, I grew up on a farm and my dad put a gun in my hands when I was eight and told me to shoot that bloody kookaburra because they don't belong here and the sooner the Victorians take them back the better off we'll all be but especially the native birds and lizards, so I know guns. But I didn't say a word. One thing I was sure about was that if a bloke came into the bank and tried to get my fifty thousand dollars I would do my best to grab my gun and shoot the prick. There was a war on and I knew lots of people didn't like it but they were communists and, like kookaburras, if we didn't stop them where they were they would take over everything. And bank robbers were just the same.

Symons took me around the building and introduced me to all the other bank johnnies, mostly expatriate Australians, but a sprinkling of local mixed race men and women and, of course, pure-blood locals who worked out the back in the storeroom and in the kitchen where they made the morning and afternoon teas and wandered around the bank with brooms and dust cloths. There were five tellers' boxes and mine was the second, number two, second in command, only one box holding more cash, number one. I was on my way. Finally, someone had taken a good hard look at me and decided I was worth something, worth a risk. I could see the headlines back home after the communist bastard had bailed me up for the fifty grand: LOCAL BOY FOILS ROBBERY ATTEMPT. RETURNS HOME A HERO.

…..

That night Robbo grabbed me naked from the shower and said: Come on, we're going to the Bulimbi Bar.

I insisted I put some non-white clothes on and when I got downstairs Robbo had his bike revved and ready. It was another mad and crazy ride out of town and along a narrow road to the bar. When he pulled up in the carpark

I fell off to one side, laughing.

When are you sandgropers going to get used to riding passenger? he said.

When are you rock-crabs going to learn how to ride a bloody motorbike?

Rock-crabs? Where did that come from?

I don't know. What do they call Queenslanders?

Bananabenders? Didn't you know?

Forgot.

New South Welsh are cockroaches. South Australians …

Yeah, I know them, croweaters.

Victorians are Mexicans. Tasmanians are two-headers. And Territorians? Who gives a shit.

We heard the music pulsing out from the upstairs windows and it got louder as we ran up the stairs. Robbo pushed the bar door open as the band finished a number and stacked its instruments for a break. The lead singer looked up as we entered and I couldn't believe the face I saw. It was Hugh bloody Bainbridge, an old, almost school chum from Grammar School, Perth's finest and most expensive private school.

He looked at me and said: Jesus Christ.

I said: Thank you, Bainers. That's the nicest thing you ever said to me.

What the blazes are you doing here, Muir?

I live here. I'm a bank johnny.

A bank johnny? You? That's a joke. If I remember correctly, numbers were not your forte.

Or my fifte.

Bainbridge was one of the A students, always in the A Class, up the top, far away from me, but he wasn't a bad bloke and he once bought me a bottle of sherry, which I threw up out a car window in the centre of Perth.

What are you doing here? I said.

My father was a lawyer, then a magistrate. Last year he was appointed Chief Justice for the island territories and he moved the whole family up with him. I'm taking a year off uni and thought I might fill in time by joining a band.

It was good news. Mum and Dad would be pleased to know I had made contact with Bainbridge, university student, son of the Chief Justice, solid citizen, member of the expatriate elite, solid Anglican and probably Rotarian. Mum's dream for her boys was that they would all marry girls from Peppermint Grove, Dalkeith or Nedlands, girls who had gone to the right and proper schools. And there seemed to be a time when I almost belonged to Perth's elite. Given I had gone to one of the city's most prestigious schools it was not surprising that I was invited to many fine and expensive parties in fine and expensive homes.

Yes, Mum, Fiona Eccleston-Blackburn has invited me to her coming-out party, I would say.

Oh, dear, that's wonderful, she would reply. Now, do behave and wear your best suit.

No, Mum, I will not.

But you must, darling. These people only wear the best. We don't want you looking shoddy and unkempt.

Mum, I'm hiring a dinner suit, with bow tie and cummerbund.

Then she'd laugh and I'd love her. I didn't always love her. Often her affectations, her pretensions, her anxiety about the small things confused and annoyed me. She was often nervous about Rotary gatherings of some sort, and often morose as if she was experiencing some kind of inner tragedy. When she was morose, I too became morose, agitated and diluted. Maybe we fed off each other, the blind taking the blind by the hand to his or her private place of misery.

Before the week was over a letter arrived from Mum with all the local news, the comings and goings that were nice and polite and seemly to mention. When I was in school Dad had often added a note at the end of Mum's, but not anymore. Maybe he had decided to leave me alone, to see how I would make my way in the world, or what the world would make of me. He did one thing I appreciated, he paid a two-year subscription to every Monday edition of *The West Australian*, Perth's only daily newspaper. It arrived once a week, one week after publication. The editor was a revered and feared man in Perth and the father of a boy in my year at Grammar School. When it arrived I took it to my room, unrolled it on the floor, turned it over then rolled it in the opposite direction to make it flat. I read papers like my father. First I flicked through, taking in the headlines and on arriving at the final page I tossed it over to the front for a more thorough reading. Inside it was packed with news from across the globe: the Vietnam War raged on; there was trouble on the Israeli–Jordanian border; students rioting in the United States; John Lennon and George Harrison were in India with an Indian guru.

In the sports pages I learnt that Lionel Rose had punched the wind out of Fighting Harada to become bantamweight champion of the world and Australia's first Aboriginal boxing champion. I was surprised, given the numbers of Aboriginal boxers in boxing tents around Australia.

Someone said it was printed on rice paper. I wondered if I could eat it.

6

My first day in teller's box number two almost convinced me I had a career in banking. I felt like the new Australian prime minister, John Gorton, who had been elected PM even though he was a senator and thus a member of the wrong house of parliament. Here I was wrongly appointed well above my capabilities, to a teller's box I didn't belong in, with a float of fifty thousand dollars, more money than I'd ever seen. I shared the box with Tom Hallett, the bloke leaving, going home after his two-year tour of duty. That's what we called it. National Service was in full force in Australia and to do your time in the islands you had to apply for a stay on your conscription papers. As soon as I headed home I'd have to let the defence department know and it would chuck my marble in the barrel and that could mean another tour of duty in another tropical climate fighting slimy Viet Cong communist bastards. Hallett was going in the barrel as soon as he got home to Melbourne. He was a tall, good-looking man and an Aussie Rules footballer. If his marble came out, he was sure to go to Vietnam.

I play for one of the local teams, he said. You interested in a game?

Yeah, maybe, I said. I wasn't too bad in school and I played a few amateur games in Perth but I'm a bit off the boil.

I'll take you down to training one night and you can see how you go.

Great.

The day was a blur. As soon as the doors opened the customer tide rushed in and didn't go out until the doors closed. All kinds trooped up to the counter: wealthy whites, drunk whites, whites in whites, whites in suits, handsome whites, very pretty whites, glorious looking blacks, blacks in whites, blacks in skirts with naked breasts, blacks with bones in their noses, blacks who stank and blacks who looked at me as though I was some kind of film star. All the while Hallett stood beside me and commented.

You see that bloke, he's worth a million. She's been around. Phil's played Rugby League down in Sydney. I saw her the other night, after the footy game, mate, she scrubs up well. Whatever you do, don't lick your fingers when counting the notes, you never know where these maries have kept their money.

What?

Yeah, that's what they call the women – maries, said Hallett. They're all called Mary and they keep their notes up their fannies.

You're bloody joking.

Nuh. You see that one down the end of the line? After you count her notes you better go and wash your hands.

I started with fifty thousand dollars, I took in over forty thousand and I handed out over twenty-five thousand and, at the end of the day, I balanced. I couldn't believe it. The old man couldn't believe it. Okay, he wasn't there, but I felt him breathing down the back of my neck, waiting for me to fuck up, to lose count, to mess the numbers up, but I didn't and inside I said a quick, silent, fuck you, you prick.

My little teller door opened. I turned and saw Symons. His hand was out, looking for mine.

There you go, he said. I had plenty of confidence in your ability to master this position. I knew you'd handle it. Knew you wouldn't let us down.

Phew, I said. Good to know I'm no John McEwen.

Symons looked at me.

You know, forced to take charge because someone died, but the wrong man for the job.

Would have been better to shove in Billy Big Ears McMahon, said Hallett. Billy might not be up for the top job either, but looking at his wife would make up for it.

McMahon had not long married a delicious woman twenty-five years younger than him and the best looking politician's wife ever. No one could explain how such a big-eared dill got to marry such a beauty, especially after so many thought he was a poofter. And no one could explain why I was still a virgin in a world gone mad with promiscuity. Not that anyone knew. It was my pathetic little secret. Along with all the others, like the lingering, occasional conversation I had with Jesus and the reason I ate so much salt.

What a day, that first one in the second teller's box. I was pumped. I needed a drink. That's the way to make euphoria last: you win a game, you get engaged, you win money, you get a pay rise – you go out and get pissed. Sober, euphoria only lasts a couple of minutes; pissed, it lasts for hours. That's what it was to be Australian. I had begun to think of myself as Australian, as belonging to a nation of people. I wondered if it had happened to the other expats, if before they had arrived they had considered themselves Queenslanders, or Victorians, but once away from our island continent, they began to think of themselves as Australians.

That whole first week in the teller's box was sweet and amazing. One night I also had another one of my flying dreams. A good one. They aren't always pleasant and sometimes I can't seem to get off the ground, no matter how hard I frog-kick or stroke with my arms. That's how I move through the air, with the breaststroke kick and stroke. It never ceases to amaze me how I do it. I never see anyone else up there with me. People look up and wave or try to get at me but they never get off the ground. In this dream I was shooting through the air, just flying, feeling the air, doing a few rolls, having fun. And when I came down Mum was waiting for me with the evening meal. She watched me land but she didn't look surprised and didn't say anything other than: Dinner's ready. I looked around for Dad but he wasn't there.

7

I couldn't believe how well everything was going. Everywhere. In Perth, the greatest Aussie Rules footballer ever, Polly Farmer, was back home and appointed captain-coach of West Perth; my brother Thomas was working in Perth as a lawyer; brother Bill was winning races and looking to be a future athletics champion; Dad had opened a new business in the town next door; and here I was straining at the bit, biting at the rope, wondering what to do now I had conquered the second teller's box. This was turning out to be my best year ever. There had to be more and bigger, brighter, better things out there for me to take on, here in the islands, at home, Europe, America, England. The world was my oyster. Maybe this was where it all started and then I'd move on to even greater success, eventually returning home triumphant: the prodigal son knocks on the door at the end of the gravel driveway, but not alone, he comes with fame, fortune and prestige, a wife, a great bundle of things they never imagined. Mum will cry, of course. Dad will look at me, in disbelief, amazement, stand back, take another look, have a think about it, check out my wife, be very impressed, then he will walk up to me, perhaps give me a traditional Italian greeting, a big man-hug with hands slapping my back. Even Jesus will weep then. What? What's he got to do with it? Shut the fuck up about Jesus. He doesn't exist, or maybe he does but not as the son of God, more likely a bloke like Gandhi, the Dalai Lama, or Herb Elliott. The longer I lived the more it looked like there was no God, but in a little piece of my brain, somewhere up the back, every so often, a conversation took place and I kept thinking it might be Jesus. Maybe I just needed someone to talk to and he was the only bloke available, even though he wasn't.

Surely Dad wouldn't be surprised by my current burst of success; after all he sent me to Grammar School. Grammar boys were destined for greatness, leadership, wealth, that was their birthright, their destiny. And look at me now, surging ahead, things appearing at my feet with very little effort. Even a mixed race girl of astonishing beauty was coming into the bank, eyeing me off, laughing at my little jokes. Maybe it was time to find out her name.

.....

Tom Hallett not only gave me his teller's box, he also gave me his carpark job at the rugby match on a Saturday night. Rugby League was big in the capital and every Saturday night the match of the day was played out in the city's major sporting stadium. All I had to do was make sure drivers parked their cars correctly, then, when the park was full, I could go into the stadium, drink beer and watch the game.

One night a Mini Minor pulled up and stopped right in the middle of the entrance. I walked over and looked in. The woman inside was beautiful, a magnificent mix of black, white and brindle. I wanted to grab her arm, catch a plane and take her home to show my racist grandfather, to show everybody, to keep her and have and hold her forever. She was crying. I tapped on the window.

You okay? I said. You want me to park your car?

She got out, still crying. I took her keys and parked her car as close as I could to the entrance of the stadium.

Thank you, she said. Her face was wet but she had begun mopping it with a handkerchief.

Is there anything else I can do? Punch some bloke? Pay off a house? Buy you an ice-cream?

She laughed. Oh, what a laugh. And that face with the laugh on it, I nearly cried. Hang on, it was her, the astonishingly beautiful woman who sometimes laughed at my jokes in the bank, who gave me a certain kind of eye, who suggested I might have a chance and here she was and I had to hand her keys back and as I did I brushed her fingers, lightly, but enough to feel her softness and to notice that she didn't recoil. She smiled.

What about I change the oil in your car, I said. Or swap your old tyres for the new ones on that car over there?

No thanks, she said. I'd better go in. My boyfriend is playing.

Then she looked at me from under her brow in a way I thought suggested sexy and walked away with a gentle sway and swish. The lizard raised its head. Her body was near perfection. Both her legs had calves. Her shoulders were straight and firm. Her long black hair floated with the swish and sway. And her arms had form, muscle, character. They were the arms of someone who had use for them. They were not limp hanging arms waiting for others to bring, to take, to do. Wouldn't I love those arms to do things for me, to me. She had a boyfriend? Which one? Which of the big galoots, the big brawny, brainless, beefy brutes?

When all the cars in the world had parked in my carpark – because that was how it seemed that night, as though everyone had decided to park their car, whatever was on, wherever they were headed, to the next town, the next country, it didn't matter, they were parking in my carpark – when they were in, I headed for the stadium, eyes peeled and burning.

The game was on. It was hard and close, white blokes, black blokes and in-between blokes, all hurling themselves at each other, punching each other, spearing each other into the dirt in a frenzy of male brutality. No finesse, nothing like the mixture of skill, poise and daring of Aussie Rules, but somehow hypnotic. I stopped looking for her, couldn't keep my eyes off the beasts as they smashed into each other, tore each other's faces off, punched each other in the neck, stomped on each other's ears in the pack. It looked like war. This, I decided, must be what it is like to face an enemy you must kill, before he kills you, an enemy, like you, whose only weapons are arms, legs and teeth.

When the game was over, the winners triumphant, the players out of the change room and mingling with the crowd around the bar, I saw her, hanging off the arm of a massive creature, the one who scored two tries by charging through three of the opposition and knocking them aside as though they were puny little blokes about my size.

8

That first week in the second teller's box was a revelation.
I had no idea I could handle so much money, or even that
I could handle money. When I wrote home I made no
mention of my success. On the Friday night we all went
over to the Pacific Hotel and drank like dogs in a spring
after a run in a desert, and then I walked back to my
little cockroach-infested room drunk, so drunk I slept the
entire night in my designated room, the room without
the massive ceiling fan and the stored documents. When
I woke up at three a.m. to piss, I got a shock, I thought
I was back home, in Genoralup, and I wondered why
the room was facing the wrong way, why it was hot, so
muggy and my arm was a mass of bulging mosquitoes
on heat and what were those soft noises like tiny things
scratching? By the time I got to the toilet, I remembered.
And when I got back to the room I decided to leave the
cockroaches to my underpants, the mosquitoes to Robbo
down the hall, and shift back to the paperwork and the
fan.

The sad thing about getting pissed on a Friday night
was that you had to get up again on Saturday morning
and work until midday. Then, of course, unless you
played sport, you could go off and get pissed again. My
Saturday in the teller's box was marred by a small error.
I finished the day fifty dollars over, but I was forgiven
quickly, because I was over and not under and because
fifty dollars in a float of fifty thousand was not deemed
a disaster.

The next week was another major success, except I was
getting a little bored. Life seemed to be all about work.
You got up, you went to breakfast, you went to work,
you bought lunch, you worked, you closed the doors, you
went to your room, you went to dinner, you went out and

got a little pissed, you went to bed. If you got a little too pissed you might have to get up and chuck your guts, you got up, chucked them, and on and on it went until you died and the mosquitoes sucked the last of your blood and the cockroaches consumed what was left and thirty-five years later someone noticed you were missing, went upstairs to the old document storage room and found your clothes and a letter from your mother reminding you to eat plenty of salt because you were once diagnosed with mercury poisoning.

By the third week the boredom was getting to me. The mixed race girl at Friday night rugby was still only smiling at me, laughing at an occasional comment, but not inviting me to share her secrets, her bed or her vagina, and my old school chum Bainbridge was about to leave town and go south.

9

There was another football match each week, the Aussie Rules game on Sunday. I went down to one training session for a look at a practice match but the sight of one local, built like a brick outhouse, roaring into one of the pasty white blokes was enough to make me flinch twice, then think. The game seemed to be a mix of rugby and Aussie Rules, some finesse, an occasional high mark, but a lot of punching, kicking, shoving in scrums and bashing, smashing, running as though their lives depended on the ball under their arms. I enjoyed it, but it wasn't like the game I knew and of the codes on offer I preferred the raw and brutal honesty of Rugby League. But when you're away from home you get all the entertainment you can and so I went to all games.

One Sunday, right after the booze-up in the clubrooms, six of us squeezed ourselves into the Volkswagen of the Bulimbi branch accountant. Jim Jackson was an older man, an alcoholic and, naturally enough, more often than not, pissed. He drove like he was pissed. What did we care? We were members of an expatriate community and expats driving pissed was normal. For most of us there was no other way to drive.

You right there? called a South Australian from the back.

The croweater, Roger, sat in the middle of the back seat. I sat on the outside, the left side, the side facing the bay, and Robbo sat on the right side, looking up the cliff face. In the front were two Victorians and Jackson at the wheel. It was a narrow road around the bay linking Bulimbi with the centre of the capital.

Too bloody right, said Jackson.

The road was wet and the rain hadn't stopped for two hours. Jackson was taking us back to the old bank quarters. Robbo and I were going out later that night to the Bulimbi Bar. My old school mate Bainers was playing his last gig and he had a hot, new, mixed race drummer in the line-up. This was a good thing and the night might well attract the drummer's sisters, their friends and their friends.

Jim was driving like a sober man. We were all laughing. All was well with the world.

You all right up front? yelled Robbo.

Too bloody right, yelled Jackson.

Jackson turned his head to show us the laughter on his face, but he turned too far, lost concentration, took a bend a little too tight, tried to correct, overcorrected, just missed an oncoming Volkswagen, overcorrected again and headed for the edge. We might have been pissed but we all knew the edge was not a good place to be. We yelled at Jackson, not so much because of the edge itself, more because after the edge there was nothing for a good twenty feet and at the bottom of the fall, on the bay floor, there was nothing but rock and an incoming tide.

Jim, yelled Robbo, we're on the fucking edge.

We hung there. No one really thought that we would go over and it looked like we wouldn't, then it did, then it didn't and then Jackson made a strange noise from his throat and his hands seemed to leave the wheel, then they took it again but moved in the wrong direction. The car shook. There was uncertainty about how much of us was on the edge, or over it. One wheel? Or two? I was sure the wheel under me was over, had been for a second or two. We seemed to hang for a long time, then a small shift, then, ever so slowly, we fell. The fall was nice. I enjoyed the fall. It was almost like flying. Someone screamed, a woman, and it was then I realised that one of the Victorians in the front was a woman. Lucky for her she was in the middle, over the handbrake. The other

Victorian, Nigel, was in front of me and as the car fell I thought, shit, I better put my elbow on the roof or a rock will come in through the window and smash my arm to smithereens, and in just the amount of time it took to think that and do it, a rock appeared at my armpit. Nigel and the Victorian woman next to him screamed, Robbo yelled, the croweater between us screamed and Jackson was silent.

On the bottom of the bay, moving quickly was important because the tide was coming in fast as it always did and lying there in a smashed Volkswagen was not a good idea. Robbo yelled at Jackson to open his door. Jackson sat slumped, gurgling.

Jackson, I yelled. For fuck's sake move.

Robbo reached over him, opened his door, pushed his seat forward then climbed out over him. Roger the croweater followed. From inside the car I helped them lift, pull and push Jackson out. He was sobbing and blubbering, apologising to everyone and offering to buy us all a drink when we got out and even take us all out for a meal. The Victorians in the front were next out and in no mood for either drink or food. The woman was helping Nigel, who was no longer screaming but moaning.

It's all right, Jim, said Robbo. Come on, we gotta get out of here because the tide's coming in and we have to get Nigel to hospital. His arm is cut up pretty bad.

Nigel's arm was in threads and blood was leaving his body in gallons whichever way he turned. The front passenger door looked like it had aimed itself for the biggest rock and most of his arm must have been on it because there wasn't much left of it where it used to be.

Here, I said, take my shirt.

The woman took my shirt and I helped her tear off a strip.

Thank you, she said. I'm June, by the way.

Great place to meet people, I thought, climbing out of a drunk Volkswagen crashed on an ocean bed with a tide racing in. I looked at her then and she wasn't too bad at all.

I'm Jack, I said, from WA.

I know. Here, help me wrap Nigel.

We wrapped the still-moaning Nigel and helped him walk across the rocks towards a place where the road and the bay bed were much closer together and where people had found a way down and were walking towards us. By now vehicles had stopped above us and some were calling out.

My wife has gone to get an ambulance, yelled a man.

Three men who had climbed down into the bay were almost with us. When they reached June and Nigel they took him back the way they had come. June turned back and grabbed at my arm.

You're hurt, she said.

No, not me.

But look.

I looked down at my arm and saw the blood and the deep cut.

Arrr, it's nothing.

What, so you West Aussies are tough, are you? Can't feel a thing, huh?

She poked her finger at the blood and I yelped.

So, you wanna go for a drink later then?

Crikey, she said. What a time to ask a girl out.

When she smiled her entire face moved, her eyebrows lifted almost to her hairline and her upper body rocked. I thought: Maybe. But it never happened. What did happen, of course, was we all went to hospital, got stitched, bandaged, released, all except Nigel, were interviewed by the police, caught a taxi to the Pacific Hotel and got so pissed we had to catch another taxi home, even though we only lived across the road. I didn't sleep that night, because not long after I went to bed under the aircraft propeller I had to get up and throw everything I had eaten or drunk over the past week into the shower recess. It stank. I stank. When I arrived at work the next morning, I stank still.

10

On the Monday, a quiet banking day, the second teller's box was out nearly five thousand dollars under and I couldn't find it. It was deemed a near disaster. Symons, the batch clerk, the senior ledger examiner, the senior teller, they all crammed into my little teller's box and squeezed me out. They found most of it, all but seven hundred and forty-two dollars seventy-eight cents. Symons was worried. He called me into his office.

Maybe you should think about curtailing your extra-curricular activities, Jack, he said.

I thought about it that night, over at the Pacific Hotel where Robbo and I got paralytic and the bar manager had to get two of the hotel boys to carry us back to our rooms. I thought about it again on Tuesday, Wednesday and Thursday, each night over at the Pacific. On Friday Symons called me into his office.

Jack, he said, you had such a good start.

Yes Richard, I said.

Are you okay?

I'm fine. I just made a big mistake.

Yes, that's clear. Look, the car accident probably affected you. It must have affected everybody on board, but you seem reluctant to curtail your nightly activities. It is very easy in the islands to get caught up in the expat lifestyle. There are not the normal restraints in place from family and social norms.

I must have looked puzzled.

Look, what I mean is, the drinking and partying. You and Robinson hang out quite a lot together. Maybe offering you a big challenge first up was not such a good idea. We should have eased you in. It's most unfortunate, Jack, but you are forcing us to make changes.

I looked away. My head was heating up. Clouds were

appearing on the horizon.

I did well the first three weeks, I said. They gave me some antibiotics up at the hospital, so my arm wouldn't get infected. Maybe they have been affecting me.

He looked at me and said nothing. His face seemed longer and narrower than I remembered. His skin smoother and shinier. Those three weeks no longer counted. Symons was about to rip it all out from under me, ignoring my success as though it had never happened. He was taking away my big break, all because of a lousy seven hundred dollars. And he was telling me who I should and should not hang out with. There was blood in my face, my neck; my entire upper body was infused with hot blood that kept pumping as I watched Symons cross a line, a line of salt I hadn't seen come up it came up so fast and there he was stepping into it, then over it. My stitches itched. You fucking shit, Symons, I screamed, you bastard, you fucking line-walker. But nothing came out my mouth.

I'm going to take you off the second teller for a week or two, give you a chance to settle in, he said. We might have been a bit premature.

That was it. I lost the second teller's box. They gave it to some punk from Tasmania, a boy who looked like he had never left home, like shaving was a mystery to him, like his mum and dad were waiting in the carpark with his lunch wrapped in greaseproof paper. Not only that, they gave him a vacant room up in the new quarters, went right by me and Robbo, didn't ask us, didn't tell us and when we went looking for him after work and couldn't find him we thought he might still be chewing on his lunch in the carpark with his parents, but no, there he was, up in the dining room along with all the others and when we asked him he said: Oh, I live here. Where do you chaps live?

43

Robbo looked at him and said: Chaps? We're down in the boondocks.

The what?

With the cockroaches.

The kid smiled. He thought we were joking.

That night we went out to the Bulimbi Bar and got well and truly pissed.

Whaddya reckon we should do now? said Robbo.

I feel a raid coming on, I said.

What? A parade? You wanna get dressed up or something?

Robbo was having trouble with his words. They were forming, but having difficulty squeezing through his lips. He didn't seem to want to open them.

I reckon we should go up to the new quarters and raid the dorms.

Dorms?

Yeah, or whatever they live in up there.

Up there, my sandgroping friend, they have new rooms like you dream about.

What, no fucking cockroaches? Bastards.

Let's get 'em.

Robbo climbed on his black Honda like it was a fifteen-hand horse, fell off, got up, and said: Here, you ride the fucking thing. It's bucking me off.

I got on. He got on and put his arms around my waist.

Not too close, I said. I'm very sensitive about blokes up my arse.

Robbo fell off again.

The new bank mess hill seemed steeper and windier than ever and it wasn't easy manoeuvring the bike with one very drunk passenger and a fairly drunk driver. But we made it. There were a few lights on but most were off.

Let's get that fucking Tasmanian, said Robbo. He's taken our room.

Our room? They were going to put us in together?

Ha ha. No, what are we, a coupla poofs?

Let's not pick on the Tasmanian, Robbo, he's got enough on his plate, you know, with his mum and dad being his brother and sister.

Jesus, you're a funny shit, Jacko.

The front door was open, so we walked in. Down the corridor between the rooms we could see lights under doors. We had no idea who lived where.

Look, said Robbo. He pointed at a fire-extinguisher on the wall.

What're ya thinking? I asked.

Nothing, just like the look of it.

He took it down and before we knew what we were doing the extinguisher was upside down and foam was hitting the wall, me, him, the ceiling and a bloke who opened his door to see what the fuss and noise was about.

What the hell do you blokes think you're doing? he yelled.

There's a fire, I yelled.

Where? he yelled.

In your room, screamed Robbo, and ran through the open door with the extinguisher shooting foam all over the man's bed and wardrobe.

Jesus bloody Christ, you bastards, yelled the man, who I could not remember seeing before and I wondered if he was a spy sent up from head office in Sydney to keep an eye on deviant expats.

The man ran back into his room and slipped on the wet floor, which gave Robbo the chance to slip out, toss the extinguished extinguisher on the floor and follow me back out the way we came.

We both tried to get on the front seat of the bike and pushed it over, allowing the inhabitants of the bank mess to stream out the door and identify their invaders.

The next day we were both called into Symons' office and told the bad news.

But first the good news, said Symons. You are not being sent home, or fired.

Thanks, Richard, I said. It was just a bit of fun that got out of hand. We were a bit upset about the Tasmanian getting a new room before us.

Yes, well, there was a reason for that. We thought it might be better for the lad to be among senior members of staff. As it's turned out, we were probably right.

And now the bad news. You are being separated, for your own good. We understand you have become good friends, but the relationship is not helping your work one iota. Robinson, you are heading off to Lua, on the other side of the island, where we have quite a large branch. And Muir, you will be going to Moroki, up in the highlands, a small branch, but one that will provide you with the opportunity to experience a wide range of banking responsibilities.

That was that. Banished. Exiled. Should I write home to the family and tell them they were right, that I had fucked up, that it was time to come home, admit my faults, face the music, and lick my wounds?

As we left, Robbo said: One good thing, Jacky boy.

What's that?

From where we're going, a trip to the Islands of Love will be a lot cheaper, and a lot closer.

Shit, Robbo. You only think of one thing.

And you, you horny little sandgroping fucker, what are you thinking of? Algebra? The price of wheat?

There was one more thing to do, go out and get pissed, which we did, straight after work.

We had a week before we got on our respective planes. And what a week it was. Every night we went out. Every night we got home late. Half the nights we chucked our guts. Every morning we were useless. And the mixed race girl, thank you Jesus, on the Saturday night, she put her face on mine.

I was late for my job at the rugby stadium. The boss was angry, but what did I care? It was my last night. There were already a number of cars in the yard and most of them were badly parked. I took my cue from them and made sure that no car parked in a designated area according to my specific instructions as laid down in the Car Parking Manual of 1957. There were cars parked in the way of other cars. I tried to cut off cars that normally left early and cars driven by people who I thought were arrogant pricks. It worked, because at the end of the night the air was full of horns. Everyone was tooting at the car in front of them, behind them, at the side of them. Some of them were stuck there a month and had food brought to them and a water tanker drove by every two days. But all that was nothing to me, because when I left for the bar, once the entire carpark was in complete chaos, she was there, the mixed race girl with the calves, the arms, the long hair and the succulent lips. Not only was she there, she was alone, looking at me, and smiling. I walked over to her.

Hello, I said.

Hello, she said.

Where's the big guy?

Who?

That man, your boyfriend.

He's gone south for a week. He's in a camp with a Sydney Rugby League club.

He didn't take you with him?

No.

He must be mad.

She touched my arm with her long fingers. Hello Lizard.

Can I buy you a drink? I asked.

Yes, she said.

I did. And then another. And more. And then, when I thought she was going to take me to her little apartment on a hill and take all her clothes off, wrestle me naked with her strong arms and rub her calves against mine and show me all the things I needed to know but hadn't seen, heard, or learnt yet, a man mountain loomed in front of me.

Diana, he said.

Her name, I had her name. And soon I'd have her and she me.

Oh, Stanley, she said.

You all right?

Yes.

Jack Muir, I said, and put my hand out.

He took it and refused to give it back. While he had it he crushed the life out of it, twisted it, turned it and just when it seemed like it might live, he crushed it again.

Stanley, he said. I'm a mate of Diana's boyfriend. You probably seen him out on the paddock.

Yes, I squealed. Then said again, from a deeper place: Yes, I seen him here, I seen him there.

Hey, aren't you the wanker who parks the cars? he said.

Oh yeah, that's me, Mr Carpark Wanker. Leave your car with me, I'll pull it off.

His face twisted a little as though confused, as though behind it there was a brain trying to grapple with a complete sentence. Just then I saw the stadium manager looking frantically around, as though anxious and irritated. The horns had started up again and seemed to be reaching new levels. I thought it might be a good idea to leave.

Well, I'd better go, I said.

Me too, said Diana. Early night.

Stanley looked at both of us.

I'll see you to your car, Di, he said.

My heart, my pants, my being, collapsed.

Hang on, I'll just go dunk Duncan in the dunny, he said.

What?

He's going to the toilet, said Diana.

He walked away. Looked back at us. We stood still. Waiting. He disappeared into the men's.

I turned to Diana and saw a look on her face that said: Kiss me. I kissed her, lightly, but her lips opened up and before I knew where I was I was inside her and she was sucking at my face but in a gentle way that enabled me to keep my general appearance and after she released me I could feel my lips again on her lips and I wanted to cry, which seemed strange, but we had to hurry because the man mountain would soon have his dick out of his mouth, back in his pants and on its way back to us, so we stopped and as we stopped he stormed up to us and we had no time to exchange addresses, numbers, handkerchiefs, underwear, all we had was the taste and smell and memory of each other.

What the fuck is it with my life, I thought, that I'm always getting great kisses just as I'm leaving a place?

One thing I learnt in boarding school: nothing was sweeter than revenge. Just before my taxi arrived at the carpark, I worked on Stanley's Vauxhall Viva. I let down the back driver's side tyre and the front passenger side tyre. My plan was that the wanker would change the driver's side first and think he was done and dusted, hop in the Viva and get a nice little surprise.

PART TWO

1

The plane is one of those turboprop Fokker Friendships, small, compact, quick. Once off the ground and the capital fades, the plane flies over rugged, jagged mountains and dense forests. The capital has no roads in and no roads out. It is an island of habitation in a sea of dense, mountainous growth. We see no sign of life, no towns, no villages, just thick and impenetrable vegetation visible through occasional breaks in the heavy cloud cover. Any people down there must be well hidden and living a life passed down unchanged generation after generation. At least until the white man came in and made his towns, his rules and flew his people all over the sky, dropping cargo at every stop, even in places where there was no need for it. And he made roads connecting towns and villages all over the islands, all except the capital. The capital remains perched and isolated on the rugged southern coastline, only accessible by sea or air.

All the way into the interior it seems as though we are on a steady climb up to our highlands destination, Moroki. I have been warned. Moroki is an outpost, a long way from the next town, home to some of the most aggressive and warlike natives, the most decadent of the expats, and the very best coffee beans.

The pilot makes his announcement. The plane dips. Out the window I see what looks like a town. We hit the tarmac hard and for one second I think we are going to roll over and my life will end before it has begun. My adult life, I mean, the life that will include the loss of my virginity.

Mr Watkins, the Moroki Colonial Bank of Australia branch accountant, greets me. The air is warm and steamy but nowhere near as hot as the capital because we are about three thousand feet up.

You must be Mr Jack Muir from Perth, says Watkins.

He puts out a soft, skinny hand that shakes mine like it is holding a banana peel. It is damp with sweat and he emits a strange, cackling noise which must be a laugh, a kind of laugh, or a man trying to laugh. His eyes glance into mine, then flick around the airport terminal.

Yes, I am, I say. You must be Mr Watkins, the branch accountant?

Yes and this is Haines. He will be showing you around the men's quarters. We don't have any women's quarters, because we don't have any women up here. Except, of course, my wife and the wife of the manager, Mr Jenson.

He cackles again and continues.

Haines will help you to familiarise yourself with our little town, its customs and the banking environment.

Another Watkins cackle as Haines puts out a firm hand that tightens its grip once it has found mine and seems to keep tightening right up until release. Haines is not holding a banana peel, he's trying to crack a walnut. I'm okay with the firm handshake and eyes that look into mine and stay there. Haines is a solid man with a straight back and broad shoulders. His pupils seem to be shrouded in a thin mist, but his hand is dry.

Gidday, he says.

How's it going? I ask.

Just about ready for the Jungle Bar.

Watkins cackles. I assume the Jungle Bar is a bar full of young men in white shirts wanting to go wild and crazy with drink. That was what they said back in the capital as they shoved me on the plane, that all there was to do in the highlands was to get pissed, fight, and fuck. I am excited about all but the fighting.

The two men don't talk much in the car and I am glad because there is so much to see out the window. The world is on the move. The roadside is full of men who look like they have been carved from the jarrah trees of my home country. Men and women walk both ways, most of them carrying something, on their backs, in their hands, or on their heads. Most of them are half naked and among them my eyes find the young girls with firm, shiny breasts. Their bodies almost excite me, but their faces don't.

You don't see much of that down in the capital, says Haines, but you don't want anything to do with them. Never know what you might pick up.

That will be enough of that kind of talk, Haines, says Watkins. He turns to me.

Richard Symons tells us that you had a bit of bother down in the capital but that you would come good.

I nod. Watkins suggests I call him Brian. I don't. Mr Watkins seems to suit him. Brian belongs to another kind of man. He is odd looking, tall, with stooped shoulders and a thin, crow-like face. Not a Brian, more a Lyndon, as in Lyndon Baines Johnson, the American president, the strange Texan who took over when JFK was assassinated.

Watkins turns into the driveway of the two-storey bank mess, where all the bank johnnies live together, eat together and sleep separately.

This is where you'll be living, says Watkins. I hope you enjoy your time here. We'll see you in the office tomorrow morning.

Haines and I get out and walk up the steps onto the small porch. I turn and wave thanks at Watkins. Haines takes me through the wide dining room, into the kitchen and introduces me to the houseboy, Tarbo, another carved young man from the other side of the mountain range.

Aftanun, says Tarbo.

I look at Haines.

He's saying good afternoon, says Haines. Up here they speak a creole, it's a mix of their native tongue, English and German.

The Germans were here?

Oh yeah. Had a great time pillaging, raping, murdering. Those were the days.

He snorts through his nose, which I imagine is a kind of laugh, then leads me upstairs and shows me to my room.

All mine? I say. Damn sight better than the crappy room I had in the capital.

Right, says Haines, I guess they had you in the old quarters then.

Yeah, the bastards. I had to shake the cockroaches out of my underpants every morning.

Haines laughs, almost a real laugh this time, but not quite, more a half-hearted laugh with his face twisted in a way that makes me think laughing is not natural for him, that it is something he has heard about, then seen on the faces of others, listened to closely and is now doing his best to imitate it.

You'll have to get to know Tarbo, Haines says, because you'll be spending some time with him.

Why's that?

Because up here we all take turns to plan the meals for a week. You sit down with Tarbo and make a list. He does the shopping, all the cooking, and he has his woman help him with the dishes. The filthy bitch lives out the back with him.

His wife?

Who knows. She's a bit feisty and every so often he has to punch her out. There's a lot of women up here like that. The highlands breeds them tough and stupid.

Where are you from, Haines?

New South Wales. Kempsey. It's up the north coast. You ever been there?

No. I dropped into Sydney on the way through and I was there about two years ago. Spent three days pissed.

That's the only way to spend Sydney.

He makes that strange snorting noise again at the end of his imitation laugh. I wonder if his nose ever leaks along with it. I've only been in the highlands half an hour, I've met two bank men, and both seem strange. I wonder what the rest of the bank johnnies are like.

Haines takes me for a walk around town. It doesn't take long. We walk to the front of the bank building, a timber bungalow, down one street past the Australian Commonwealth Bank, our major and only competition, one of the ubiquitous Byrne Brothers Trading Stores, then through a bush track to the other side of town and past the Jungle Bar and its home, the Highlands Hotel Motel. All the way around town there is an endless stream of natives walking by from both directions.

Where are they going? I ask.

Who knows, says Haines. They probably don't either and I don't care. When the other blokes finish the day we'll take you over to the Jungle Bar and introduce you to the expat population. Most of them are in there after work and some of them don't leave until they are carried home by their houseboys.

Any chicks around? I ask.

Plenty, but not the colour you'll want. There's a few nurses up at the hospital and lots of expat wives, including a couple who like to lick young blokes now and again.

Another snort and this time he shows his teeth. They are not pretty. I imagine them ripping into raw flesh.

So what do you do for entertainment?

We've got a table tennis table we put up in the dining room a couple of days a week, mainly Saturday after lunch, and Sunday. There's always snooker down at the Moroki Club. We'll get you signed up. Not much else really. There's no TV, of course. Every so often someone comes by with a projector and a porno movie. In the school holidays young chicks come home from boarding school down south, but they're usually snobs and won't have anything to do with us bank johnnies. Oh, and there's always the occasional punch-up offered by Tarbo when he lays into his wife.

You watch that?

There's nothing on the telly.

Haines snorts. His lips are set in a sneer, every so often parting to show his bad teeth. He's from northern New South Wales. Maybe he's caught between the swagger of a Queenslander and the innocent ignorance of an outback country town. He leaves me in my room and heads back to work.

Everyone in the mess has a room to himself and, joy of joys, so far, no sign of cockroaches. My room is new, clean and I'm on the top floor. I walk out onto the upstairs veranda and breathe in the moist air full of tropical fragrances. It's a sweet smell, nothing like the rotting stench of the capital. I lie on the bed and wonder how I got there: I'm a boy from the West Australian bush, from an old South-West family steeped in tradition, sent to one of Perth's most prestigious schools, where I failed badly, then forced to work in a bank and now I'm here in a highlands branch in a country not yet a nation, more a colonial remnant. I'm also a virgin. Something has to give.

When the bank closes the other blokes straggle over and hang out in the dining room with stubbies of beer in their hands. There are seven of us altogether. Everyone has a nickname. Haines is Hanno. I'm Jacko. Franky and Hanno are from New South Wales. Timbo from Victoria. Prem and Holden from South Australia and Nippy from Tasmania.

We eat pork chops, sweet potato, peas and a mess of other things I don't recognise. After dinner we move the tables and chairs aside, bring out the table tennis table, play a round robin, dismantle the table tennis table, Haines tells Tarbo to put the tables and chairs back where they were and we all drift off to our rooms.

This what happens every night? I ask Haines.

No, he says, some nights we tell Tarbo to dismantle the table tennis table.

I go back to my room and open my latest copy of *The West Australian*. Back home we would fight over the daily paper. One of the few things Dad and I had in common was a curiosity about the world. ABC news bulletins, the *Daily News* and *The West* barely satisfied our thirst.

I settle in to read every single item in the paper. I have the time. The Aussie Rules football season is about to start, Robert F. Kennedy has entered the US presidential race, and students in Europe and America are still protesting, taking over buildings and getting the shit beaten out of them by angry policemen. I'm still not sure why the students are running amok and I fear for Kennedy. I will never forget waking up in boarding school, hearing the news of his brother's assassination and bawling my eyes red. I fall asleep and dream I'm flying again, on my own, propelling myself along with a breaststroke-like action.

2

My first day at work is a shock. The building is too small for all of us. We are packed in tight, with very little room to stretch. The four big propellers in the ceiling are low, low enough to make me think twice about stretching my arms. As I walk in, I feel like walking out.

Jenson the manager calls me into his office.

Would you mind, Muir, he says. This way, please.

It is clear to me that he is not a man to ask me to use his first name and he won't have any interest in mine. His stomach hangs over his long pants. He is the only man on staff not showing his legs. The rest of us are in the standard whites: short-sleeved shirts, shorts, long socks. Jenson's face is red, fleshy and in the middle of it is a nose you worry about, pink and full of swollen veins.

Muir, he says. We have your report from the capital and it appears as though you need a break from handling money. No teller's box for you. We only have two and they contain two of our most efficient bankers. You will be on the statement machine.

I beg your pardon, Mr Jenson? Did you say statement machine?

Yes. You may have noticed, Muir, there are no females in this branch. All the work is done by men. You are a man and a statement machine operator. We'll see how you go.

Thank you, Mr Jenson. If the statement machine doesn't work out, what else is on offer?

He looks at me.

It came down the grapevine, Muir, that you have a sense of humour.

Jenson doesn't smile, or laugh and although I say thank you it is not what I mean. Fuck you, pumpkin face, is a lot closer. I walk out of his office with a warm head.

Statement machine? This is girls' work. I am not a girl. I am a man. I want a girl.

Watkins is waiting for me outside. He takes me to my machine.

There she is, he says and cackles.

I hear a snort. Haines, somewhere behind me. Franky the ledger machinist gets up from his machine and says: Welcome to my world.

I'll leave you in Frank's capable hands, says Watkins.

I look down at the brute. She has no shape, no form, she is a huge, green, stinking lump of metal.

You're not too keen, are you? says Franky.

Shit, mate, I say. What the fuck has the world come to?

Listen, it's not as bad as you think. We get to sit down all day and if we balance early, we go home early. All we have to do is agree with each other.

What's the stench?

It's her oil. We have to grease her.

What?

Franky laughs like a man born to laugh.

Is that all we have to do? I ask.

There's one more thing.

We don't have to fuck her too, do we?

Franky throws his head back. I am liking Franky already. He seems normal.

No, but we have to help Timbo out on the enquiry counter. And that's got good points.

Yes?

And bad points.

What are they?

We get to get up and walk.

Yeah.

And talk to some of the young and attractive women in town.

Really? All three of them?

No, there are others. They may be different colours, but they are still attractive.

And the bad points?

Sometimes the enquiries are complicated and they take time and sometimes the customers stink and you have to stop breathing.

Franky grins at my discomfort and I sit in the chair at my machine and know I don't care how many good-looking women there are, I only need one of them to take me, hold me, kiss me, teach me. It has to happen. Time is running out. My virginity has to go before Robert F. Kennedy is president of the United States of America or before he is shot down like his brother, or before I get killed by an angry father, or get transferred to an outpost in the middle of nowhere, which is probably over the next hill, or before I am shot by invading communists while trying to save the town because then the fathers of Moroki will throw their daughters at me and I have to know what to do with them when they land in my lap.

Franky gets to work, teaching me everything there is to know about operating a statement machine. He doesn't let me off the hook. I get all the detail. My head aches, but I stay with him.

You pick up the entry, he says, whether it is a cheque, a withdrawal, or a deposit form. You find the account name. You then grab the statement that corresponds with that account name and you place it in the machine. You add the previous balance, add or subtract the entry, bingo, the machine does the rest.

You're a genius, Franky, I say.

I feel stupid, my father's voice comes at me from the back of my head: You must concentrate, apply yourself. This is a simple task that even your mother could do. That's a bit fucking much. We both know my mother couldn't. She never worked again after the war. They got married in 1946 on discharge from the armed forces, and lived happily ever after. Well, he was armed, she wasn't. Mum was a nurse at the rehabilitation hospital in Shenton Park and I once heard her tell a friend that she worked in a ward full of men with infected penises, all sent home from the Middle East. I've always wanted to ask her if that was where she met Dad. I know it wasn't, of course, but I want to ask, just once, to get back at her for something, anything. I'll find a reason. The outside world is foreign to Mum. A statement machine would confuse her, scare the shit out of her, send her scurrying and dropping tears all the way to her bedroom. I want to do the same, right now, run from the bank, up to my little cockroach-free room in the bank mess, slam the door and not come out until a mixed race beauty cajoles me, entices me, seduces me and promises me she would not only have passionate, naked sex with me but she'd also work the statement machine.

I don't run and she never comes. I get down to it. I concentrate. I work the machine. I fall in love. We live happily ever after. No, that never happens.

It's the end of the day. Frank looks at me.

You done? he asks.

I don't know, I say. You better check.

He does. Another miracle. Our numbers agree. We put things away in our little drawers and head over to the Jungle Bar.

Where you from in New South Wales, Franky? I ask.

Wollongong, he says.

What are you doing up here?

I work in a bank, he says. I'm a career bank johnny. What about you?

I have no idea.

Franky takes a long hard drink.

Wollongong is a coal mining town. There was only ever two places to work in the Gong: the coal mine or the steelworks. My dad worked in the mine and he always said it was the last thing he wanted me to do so he made sure I finished high school. When I get home I'll keep going with my accounting studies.

My dad would like me to do that, I tell Frank.

You don't look the accounting type, Jack.

Thanks, Franky, that's the nicest thing anyone ever said to me.

We order another beer and then the rain starts.

Every night the same, says Frank. We better have another five then it won't matter how wet we get.

We run back to the bank mess, arrive soaking wet and find all the others waiting. It looks like someone is going to say grace, but no, they just want to welcome me, the new boy. I thank them. Frank and I sit and eat as water runs off us onto the floor and Tarbo comes out with a towel and mops up around us. I get up to help but Frank pulls me back.

The meal is delicious, a big plate of sweet potato, pork, beans and some other vegetables I can't find a name for.

3

I have been hard at it for two weeks now. I have found my rhythm and tried hard to concentrate on the bank forms, the deposits, withdrawals. I pull the statements carefully from the tray on the trolley, making sure the account names match the names on the forms, find the relevant numbers, enter them, take a breath, move onto the next. That is all it takes, concentration, nothing more, I try hard to contain my excitement, all it takes, concentration, on every small piece of paper in front of me and all the large yellow sheets of paper beside me. Must make sure my stumpy little fingers stay connected to my eyes and find the right numbers to punch on the keyboard. Stay calm, don't move too fast. I have reached the pinnacle of my banking career. There is nowhere to go from here.

One thing is clear to me, the statement machine operator position is a job designed by someone who thought that at the end of the Second World War there were too many women who needed to move aside from sensible jobs to make way for men coming home. They need extra jobs they can go to, this person thought. What we'll do is take the statement away from the ledger. They are the same entries, yes, but why not make two jobs where one would be plenty? We can put the statement and the ledger together, with some carbon in the middle, one entry for both, that would make sense, but why do that with all these women needing to move on, to find new work? There is one major flaw in his idea: he has not considered that in certain towns, in particular those towns bereft of women, the work will be done by men, and these men will hate him for it, resent it, rebel against it and, eventually, seek him out, find out where he lives, bomb his house and hang him by his neck until he begs for forgiveness.

I maintain my sanity with regular visits to the enquiry counter. When I arrived, Timbo the Victorian was the enquiry clerk, but he got sick because he forgot to take his malaria tablets, and he's now on a plane home. There is no replacement. Franky and I have to fill the gap. It saves my arse. I make a deal with Franky that I will take on the bulk of the enquiries if he helps me find my slowly increasing number of errors. That's how it is with me: when I start something I look great, like I've got everything under control, like I'm some kind of genius, then I get bored, the shit piles up against the fan, I lose all interest and find myself moving on, or being told to move on. Same thing happened in the capital: great start, got complacent, got bored, fucked around and fucked up. It shouldn't happen, not after all those years I was groomed to succeed. But it does. Franky likes the idea of me taking on the enquiry counter because he isn't fond of the job, the endless procession of people with questions about bank opening times, about forms long dead, about deposits they were sure they had made and withdrawals they were sure they had not. Enquiry counter doesn't look very exciting on paper, or sound very exciting when you say it out loud, but it is for me, because I get to get up out of my chair and walk, and talk, and meet some of the wildly attractive and sexy local girls. There is one exception, a nurse from South Australia, who comes in once a week to bank her cheque. Franky has the hots for her. Whenever Jenny comes in Franky gets the counter. Even if I am there, standing, having just completed a previous enquiry and she stands right in front of me. I excuse myself, turn, wink, and Franky jumps up from his great machine, a much bigger monster than mine, and runs to the counter. It is all unnecessary, of course, because she could bank her cheques with one of the tellers, but up here, in the highlands, we have to make our own excitement and take it as often as we can.

Then there's the books. I have always been a great reader. My school days were full of reading, history mainly, but I loved a good adventure story. Once I got through *Treasure Island*, *The Coral Island*, *Moby-Dick* and others, I headed for those tomes full of sex and mayhem. The first sex-charged novel I ploughed through before I finished high school was *Peyton Place* and it disappointed me. Yes, there was sex, but not enough of it and no adventure. Just a bunch of randy folk in a town. Then there was Harold Robbins; he knew how to juice a young man's groin. I didn't bring any books with me. I was expecting to spend my two years in the capital where there was a library and a trading store with a small collection of books for sale. In Moroki there is no library and no shop with books, but one of the tellers, Paterson, or Prem, is a big reader and his brother sends him a new book every month. The first book he hands me is the Robbins masterpiece, *The Adventurers*.

It's Harold Robbins at his best, says Paterson.

No one can tell me why Paterson is called Prem. He arrives with Prem, they call him Prem and he leaves with Prem.

Then there's Dorothy Sogata.

I am sitting at the Beast. A new sheet has just gone into her slot. And Dorothy Sogata enters the building. Every bank johnny in proximity looks at her, aiming for a smile. She obliges. She is short, of course, they're all short, but she has a swagger, a gait, a feminine swing and flow and a face that oozes something, fun, joy, and other things I hope to find out. Dorothy has kissing lips and hips that I imagine are perfectly designed for whatever hips do when they do it, make love, have sex, whatever it is called when it happens but, dear Jesus, please let it happen.

The office belongs to Dorothy Sogata. The manager, Jenson, appears at his door, notices Dorothy, blushes, and returns to his den. Haines snorts from somewhere in the stationary cupboard.

I fall out of my chair because I can see she is headed for the enquiry counter, and I want to be there as she arrives. Franky gets out of his chair.

Back off, Franky, I say, this one is mine.

You bastard, he says, grins and sits.

Dorothy has seen the interaction. She is ready for me.

Good morning, I say.

Her eyes take in mine, then the rest of me and she says: You are new.

Yes, I say. And so are you.

Only for you, she laughs, a laugh that sends a shudder all the way down to the lizard.

Can I help you? I ask.

Of course, she says.

Then she tells me what she requires and almost as soon as she is finished I have to ask her to tell me again, as I have not concentrated on her words, I have concentrated on the lift of her chest, the movement in her face, the shift in her shoulders. And her eyes. I can see another world in there and it is screaming at me: Come!

When I sit back at the Beast, Franky leans across the short space between us.

Jack, he says, it's okay to laugh and flirt, but don't go any further.

Frank, I say, I'm a virgin. She'd eat me alive.

I can see he doesn't believe me. I drop my head quickly and return to the forms stacked in front of my machine. I don't want Franky to see the red creeping over my face.

Dorothy comes in at least once a week. She always finds a reason to front the enquiry desk. When she leaves the building, I go back to the Beast and when the Beast is done for the day, I join most of the others as they head over to the Jungle Bar. Within three weeks, Franky and

Prem propose me as a member of the Moroki Club. On my first visit I see a club right out of Somerset Maugham. It is a large rambling building set up high overlooking a golf course. It is late in the day and the veranda is full of men sitting in wicker chairs, smoking, drinking and looking out over a world they command. When their glasses are empty, they call, Boy, and a native man brings them another full glass. As the afternoon winds on, more and more slur their words, until, finally, small groups of two and three stumble to their cars or Land Cruisers and drive erratically towards the main road into town. That first day in the club I play snooker with Haines and beat him. He doesn't like it but pretends he does and buys me a beer. I don't like it, the beer, but pretend I do. It's called Banda Beer and is imported from the Philippines.

Watkins is not a member of the club, but Jenson is, although we don't see him. No one likes Watkins. He is a classic conscientious accountant, picky, pedantic and forever sober. There is no long lunch with Watkins. In my first six weeks I only see him have one drink.

4

One day we all balance early, at around the same time, and Watkins decides we should have a beer at the office. Jenson is down south for a meeting of bank managers and Watkins is a bit full of himself as the acting manager.

All right, says Watkins, gather around, staff. I thought it might be nice if we have a drink and toast our good fortune. I have instructed Timmy to purchase us all a bottle of Banda Beer for that very purpose.

Timmy is the office boy. He runs errands, makes cups of tea and coffee, cleans the offices and walks around with a cloth in his hand, endlessly wiping, brushing and collecting miniscule items of rubbish. We all look at Watkins as though he is a complete gimp and he is. As soon as the beer arrives we scull our bottles and leave Watkins alone in the office with half a bottle of Banda in his hands, cackling like an idiot. As we leave the building, Holden Higgs comes out of the toilet.

It's you and Watkins, Higgs, says Haines. You think you can handle him? Tell him about the disc brakes on the HD Holden and the new Powerglide automatic transmission unit.

Holden Higgs' face lights up, just for a second, until he realises Haines is taking the piss.

You'll keep, Haines, says Higgs.

Haines laughs and leads us over to the Jungle Bar where we get pissed as farts and stumble home in the rain. Most nights we head off to the Jungle Bar, but not Watkins, every night he goes straight home to Mrs Watkins and the two little Watkins. Wato we call him, but not to his face, then it is Mr Watkins. I should admire him for keeping to his beliefs, his code, but there is too much to annoy me: his irritating cackle, his pretended efficiency, his distance and smugness. He believes he is a first-class accountant, but he isn't.

It's not him, says Franky. It's the ledger examiner, Higgs. Higgs makes him look good. Higgs might be a smug prick too, but Higgs has good reason, because he is efficient, smart and he knows the name of every form ever produced or currently used by the bank and their particular purpose and he knows the manual inside out, back to front, side to side, and, would you believe, in German.

German? I ask. Really?

No, says Franky, just thought I'd chuck that in.

He's not alone, adds Franky. But while we, the regular bank johnnies, might have been chosen for our potential, the managers and accountants up here in the islands have been chosen because their potential has expired, or never existed. It's like head office has realised people like Jenson and Watkins have risen above their capabilities and the only place left to send them is the islands, where they will be beyond causing harm because of the excellent staff around them. There are exceptions, of course.

Franky looks at me and grins.

.....

Why are you always up at the enquiry counter, Jack? asks Watkins.

What do you mean, Mr Watkins?

The enquiry counter position is a shared position, yourself and Frank. Frank, perhaps you can explain?

Well, says Frank, we just thought it was a job more suited to Jack's talents than mine, Mr Watkins.

Such decisions in the future will be made by myself, or Mr Jenson. Is that clear?

Yes, sir, Mr Watkins.

Please restore the status quo, Frank.

Of course, Mr Watkins.

As he lopes away, Franky and I give him the two-fingered salute.

5

Haines is right about the school holidays. Hordes of young high school girls descend from the skies and make their way to local parties. They come home from boarding school, mainly Brisbane, but some from even more exclusive Sydney boarding schools. One is the white daughter of a local plantation owner. Her name is Elizabeth Johnson. She is tall, blonde, strong-limbed and she oozes sex. At least that's what I think it is and what Franky says it is and Franky lives in a big city not far from Sin City, Sydney.

It is, says Franky. It's sex. You can see she's ready. Can't you see it?

Of course, I say, with the blood already rushing to my face, knowing I have no idea what sex looks like when you aren't doing it, or even if you are doing it, or what it looks like on a girl's face if she wants to do it, or has done it, or thinks you are the one to do it with. I know what it looks like on my face when I'm doing it, alone, just me and the lizard, because I have done it in front of a mirror. But not since I have been in the highlands. Too drunk, too hot, and maybe I'm saving myself.

The one thing I do know is that when they laugh I am in for a shot at the prize. I am in luck: Elizabeth Johnson thinks I'm funny. One night, after the Jungle Bar closes, we all wander off in the rain and finish up at somebody's house, a house I have never been in before. It has the look and stench of a colonial mansion and sits on the edge of town. It must have belonged to a big man, a coffee plantation owner, a district commissioner, certainly a major colonialist, but time has taken him and left his mark. There are rooms all over the place. Late in the night, when Liz and I are well and truly free of any inhibitions, she drags me away from the crowd, down corridors, onto verandas, into the rain, then back into rooms, many already populated with tangled couples, until we find one that suits us, a long way from all the others. It has a single bed and a desk. Liz pushes me onto the bed and begins ripping her clothes off. I can't believe it. She is so eager. She not only oozes it, she demands it. I have heard stories of eager girls but I have never met one, or seen one in front of me, or witnessed the frantic tearing of clothes.

Come on, she yells.

She jumps up and begins tearing at my clothes. I want to kiss her. She allows me to kiss her while removing my pants but all that happens is my lips punch hers but mainly hit her nose, and her lips make no attempt to get to mine. Then she lays back, grabs at my overexcited lizard and pulls it towards her. She keeps pulling me and thrusting her groin, but we aren't getting anywhere. My lizard keeps hitting a solid wall of flesh. She is closed. I have no idea what is wrong, why we can't achieve entry, why she can't open up and let me in. I know I have to get in, that the man enters the woman, but where, how? She must know, surely, where her vagina is. I say nothing. I close my eyes. I leave the discovery process to her, I think it best, think she will know where to put the lizard. He is only able to take so much pulling and thrusting without entry and I can feel the pressure building and him getting ready and the more ready he gets the harder I thrust and the more she pulls the more excited he gets and then, with very little warning, just a sudden thrill from somewhere deep in the groin and along the lizard length, he gives himself up, all over her, or where he thinks she might be and when he is empty and done, we lie still.

I'm sorry, she says.

That's okay, I say.

I don't know what happened. Maybe you're too big.

I know I'm not. I have seen enough width and length in boarding school and football club showers to know I am a long way off too big but it is nice to hear someone say it.

What's the time now? she asks.

I don't know, I say, maybe eleven-thirty.

Shit. I'd better get home. My dad freaks if I'm not home before midnight.

She wipes my seed off her stomach with a bedsheet, gets up, puts on her clothes, kisses me and says: You want to see me again?

Of course, I say.

But I don't mean it. She is young, probably jail bait, a little too eager for me and I can't get in. It was good the lizard missed because a direct hit might mean a man at my door with a shotgun followed by a weeping wife and mother and a reverend with a Bible and that would be the end of me, trapped in a marriage I didn't plan and didn't want. I'd be a good husband and father, at first, then all would go wrong. That's how it goes with me. What chance would a poor bastard born of my seeds have with a father like me? None. What I need is someone older, wiser in the ways, someone who can get me in, someone not so eager, someone who knows how to protect herself.

6

It's Saturday afternoon. Lunch is eaten and the debris cleared away. We bring out the table tennis table. Some of the blokes go up to their rooms to read, write home, or wank. I toss up the options. I decide to play Haines again. I thrash him again. When the final point is mine Haines throws his bat into the kitchen.

Easy, Hanno, I say. It's only a game.

Get fucked, Muir, he says, then he trudges up the stairs to his room for a wank, to read *Mein Kampf,* or to rip the wings off small birds, I have no idea, but it is becoming clear to me that Haines is not like the rest of us. Neither am I, but he inhabits some other place where none of us wants to go. Paterson and I play each other until we collapse in a heap of sweat and laughter. Paterson is good. We hear a commotion outside. We jump up to see Tarbo beating his wife. She is not happy.

Hey, Tarbo, yells Paterson.

Tarbo turns and as he does his wife picks up a bottle and smashes it over his head. He falls to the ground screaming, head in hands, and by the time Paterson reaches him his hands are full of blood. I run to the phone to call Watkins because we don't have a car. Paterson and I do what we can to stop Tarbo bleeding, while his wife cries and smacks her head with her fists. When Watkins arrives I get in the car with him and Tarbo. As we leave I see Haines on the veranda outside his room, watching, laughing. At the hospital we take him in the wrong entrance, the white entrance, and have to take him around the back to the black entrance. It isn't called the white entrance, or the black entrance, there are no signs, but the nurse in the front office says we have to take him around the back.

That's where the natives go, she says.

We leave him there and Watkins drives me back to the bank mess. When I walk in no one seems too worried about Tarbo. I have a beer with Paterson and ask him why he is such a good table tennis player.

I played competition table tennis back home, he says.

Serious? I ask.

Do I look serious?

No.

Well I am. Played for Glenelg in the city league.

You're joking? The city league?

Yeah, we take our table tennis seriously in Adelaide.

Along with your footy, your churchgoing, wanking, drinking and probably because there's nothing else to do in Adelaide.

You bloody sandgropers can't get over the thrashing we hand out in interstate footy.

Having your hand in sand isn't anywhere near as primitive as eating crows.

And so it goes, back and forth, one after the other, along with the ping-pong ball, because after the beer we decide to play one more game and the blokes who are left stand back and marvel at the skill of a Glenelg league player and a wiry little bastard who learnt to play in a boarding school. Paterson doesn't ask me why I am so good but if he did I would tell him it is because in boarding school I hated losing to big kids who thought they were good at everything, and in the highlands I hated losing to South Australians, Victorians, anyone from over the other side of the black and burnt stump.

Tarbo walks into the kitchen with a large bandage on his head.

Fixim pretty good? asks Paterson.

Yes, masta, says Tarbo.

I look at the makeshift bandage and think: Probably

wasn't a doctor who stitched and bandaged him, more likely a nurse, or some old woman out the back who had a ball of string.

7

It's Saturday night. There's a bucks party; one of the local coffee buyers is getting married. His name is Peter Fraser and his family banks with us at the Colonial. He invites us all to join him down at the little hall on the edge of town.

The hall is much like a small town hall anywhere in Western Australia, flat timber floor, timber walls, drab curtains, small kitchen at the back and an outside toilet. Tables full of food line one wall, buckets full of ice and beer line the other and a boiling urn full of frankfurters sits on a small table near an electric power socket. There are no speeches. Blokes walk between one wall and another, picking up beer, food and frankfurters. Finally, a bloke who says he is Frasey's best mate stands up and says: Right, let's get this show moving. Two blokes erect a screen in front of the frankfurter urn and another brings out a movie projector. Light flickers on the screen. Someone pulls curtains. The hall lights go out. There is no sound, but we see a bloke enter a room where two women sit on a bed. They offer him lollies. He sucks a lolly. One of them puts her hand inside her panties. The other puts her hand on his crotch, then begins to rub his penis. She opens his fly and puts her hand inside. He stands, removes his clothes and they remove theirs. They play with each other's genitals. The blonde woman sucks his dick. The brunette sucks the blonde's vagina. They swap. Then they all shift and the blonde puts his dick in her vagina, while the brunette rubs the blonde's tits. The open vagina seems huge and the man's lizard enters with ease. Blokes are screaming and laughing. My lizard is growing. The screen flickers, the film stutters, flutters and stops. The projector is silent. Blokes yell. Someone strikes a match. There's a crash. A light comes on. Frankfurters are rolling on the floor. Blokes are laughing their heads off. Someone throws a frankfurter, then another, and then the air is full of flying frankfurters. One hits me on the forehead. I grab a plastic bottle of tomato sauce and squeeze it into Haines' pocket. He turns and takes a swing at me. I duck and laugh but keep him in sight just in case he takes another shot. Franky is wearing a ring of frankfurters around his neck.

This reminds me of the annual Coalminers' Ball, he yells. Someone hits him in the chest with a shot from a sauce bottle.

The hall is alive with flying food. Haines has a bottle of sauce and he squirts it in my face. A curtain is on fire. Then all the curtains are in flames. Someone yells: Fire! Fire! Everyone laughs. We spill out into the yard. The wooden hall is in flames. We stand and laugh and watch it fall into itself. The police don't come. The fire brigade doesn't come. I wonder if it is because they are here already, that among our number are men from the police and the fire brigade. We stumble home to the bank mess and I go into my room and wank into a hanky.

8

Pressure is building. My testicles are sore and my lizard is tired of handling. It dreams of entry, the imagined soft pleasures of all-encompassing wet flesh, internal flesh. And the Beast is killing me. I have tried to get used to her, to like her, at least to tolerate her, to no avail. I run tests on her, oil her, do all I can to ensure she is safe and happy. It doesn't work. She gives me the shits, or nothing. I am beginning to loathe her. She embarrasses me. I write home but make no mention of work. As far as they are concerned I am happy as Larry. I want to be happy as Larry. I want to find Larry and live with him because if anyone can fix me up with the right girl, it must be Larry. Some of me is sometimes happy. I feel a kind of happiness when I beat Haines at table tennis but it isn't real happiness. It smells a lot like the revenge of an angry man. And too often when I am alone in my room dark clouds roll in with the evening rain after yet another meal smothered in salt and laden with sweet potato, pork, and other vegetables I am still to learn the names of. Then I open the latest copy of Perth's one and only and finest Monday morning newspaper, wondering how I messed up the second teller's box down in the capital and why it matters to me because I am not intent on a career in banking, or anything else. I have a small salt shaker in my cupboard. I shake salt out of it most mornings when I get up and most nights before I go down.

Monday's *West Australian* arrives every week, never on a Monday and never the same week as publication, so all the news is old but welcome. American Negroes are still marching for their rights, President Lyndon Johnson says he will not seek re-election for the presidency of the United States and John Gorton clings on as prime minister of Australia.

When I'm done with the paper I settle down with the great adventure writers Harold Robbins, Alistair MacLean and Leon Uris. Robbins, in particular, encourages me because his characters always seem to have such tough early times, then good times, followed by bad and finally good. Something always comes up. A new woman. Sudden outbreaks of riches. And his main men are real men; they know how to break another man's leg with a quick flick of an arm or punch with a fist, twist a neck to kill instantly, and take a woman who doesn't want to be taken and make her happy because of it. I will wait for it, the something to come up. It must. Eventually. There is no way I am leaving early, not before I have more of whatever it is that comes up, and sex, there must be sex. I cannot leave without sex, I have promised the lizard sex, real sex, the sex of man in woman. Even if there is a God and he doesn't like it, I must have it. Marriage is out of the question. I'm with the revolting students on this, the free love, the freedom to fuck outside official sanction. The only difference between me and them is that they are getting it and I am not.

9

We are all invited to another party, this one up at the nurses' quarters, once again the entire bank johnny contingent. What are we now, party guests for people with no friends? Invitations are received, dress code included and we are asked to bring our own alcohol. I wear my grey suit and carry a bottle of vodka. I am in a vodka mood and, besides, Banda Beer is shit.

The nurses must be desperate to invite all of us, I mean, half of us are of no value, are not interested, no fun, don't drink, and have no idea how to behave around women. How do I know this? Franky told me.

We walk to the hospital quarters because, for once, it isn't raining. Every so often the nights are warm and balmy and dry. This is such a night and we are all in good spirits. Even Higgs is with us. We don't know why. His chances of finding a nurse to discuss the Holden HK Monaro are remote, or even the wonders of the Holden EH with its seven-bearing crankshaft and hydraulic valve lifters. Every so often we can't stop him and he lets loose over the pork and sweet potato. One night Paterson made a big mistake and asked him why the HD was such a disaster. Three hours later when I came downstairs for a cup of Milo, Higgs was still droning on about disc brakes, camshafts and bucket seats.

We are greeted at the nurses' quarters by a senior looking lady and shown into a room. The room is empty, except for a few chairs, a table with white tablecloth and a fridge in one corner. It looks like a training room.

The girls are on their way, says the senior lady.

Someone says, Thank you.

You can put your drinks in the fridge, she says.

We put them in, then take them out. We think we are thirsty after the hard morning at the bank.

We hear a door open and a new voice says, Hello.

We all turn. She is black. And beautiful.

Oh, hello, too many of us say at the same time.

I'm Margaret Baker, she says. I'm not a nurse, but some of my friends are. They invited me here tonight.

I can't speak. I want to speak, but I can't. There is a sound deep inside me trying to get out but I won't let it because it might sound like a wild animal on heat and that would not be a good look in front of Margaret Baker with her small neat breasts pushing against a blouse, arms with form and the unmistakeable outline of muscle, legs showing under a dress and clearly built for running up and down sandhills.

My voice returns.

Hello, I say. I'm Jack Muir. I'm not a nurse either.

Margaret Baker laughs. I hear music. I try not to stare at her beauty, to gawk, to remove my clothes, to remove hers, to run naked with her then lie in an exhausted tangle with our limbs and sweat mixing and merging. I stand very still. Some of the others still gawk. There is an awkward group-gawk moment. It is relieved by a noise behind her. The music stops. The door opens and before anyone can say Dave Clark Five the room is full of nurses, white nurses, in coloured dresses. Even when they gather around her and she turns towards them, she does not disappear among them, not because she is black and they are white but because she is beautiful and articulate and striking and I think I could love her because, there seems no doubt, she is the princess of my dreams.

The senior nurse, the one we met earlier, begins introducing herself and the others. I meet them all, including Franky's favourite, the South Australian, who is nice, plain, probably a churchgoer and maybe even a coalminer's daughter. I remember none of their names, except Margaret Baker's. And Jenny's, and I only remember Jenny's because I have heard it a thousand times from Franky.

The night seems over before it starts. I think I'm pissed. Maybe it is the five rum and cokes I had before I arrived. Maybe I should have used more orange juice with the vodka. I know I want to take Margaret Baker away with me to love and hold until death rips us apart, but when I go looking for her she is gone. I can't believe I let her out of my sight. I had to let her out of my sight, to save us both the embarrassment of my gawking.

Where's Margaret Baker? I ask Jenny.

Her father collected her about ten minutes ago, she says. She's still in school, you know, and her father doesn't let Margaret out for long. You can probably see why.

Jenny smiles and I smile and then the red rushes to my face. I make a noise that I hope sounds like a laugh and bend down to retie my shoelaces and Jenny laughs, probably because she can see the red at the back of my neck.

Yes, I say. Does she live out of town?

Her father runs a coffee plantation a few miles out, says Jenny. He was a district officer for many years, fell in love with a local woman, they got married and had two kids who both go to exclusive schools in Sydney.

Right, I think, that cuts me out. She's too good for me.

Margaret reminds me of Penelope Bickford, a girl from Genoralup, not because Penelope is black – she's whiter than me – but because she is destined for great things. Penelope left high school, went to university and the last letter from home carried the news that she is finishing her degree at George Washington University and has a holiday job at the United Nations in New York. Whenever Mum writes, there is always mention of Penelope this or Penelope that, alongside news of my older brother, Thomas, of course, the big-shot lawyer in Perth.

I go to the fridge, grab a bottle of something, rum I think, not sure, don't care, drink it like it is lemonade, head back to the bank mess in the rain that arrives late and is making up for it, plummeting down in great bundles of wet. I don't run, sort of stumble, my head on fire, get to my room, swallow the salt shaker, throw myself on the floor, get up, throw my clothes on the floor, fall onto the bed, cough up a salt shaker, watch the room spin, life spin, get out of bed, too late, throw everything on the floor. I wake up with my face stuck in a pool of bile still trickling out one corner of my mouth.

10

Two days later, someone hears it on Radio Australia: Martin Luther King the American civil rights leader is assassinated. Before I go to sleep I cry. I remember crying when President Kennedy was shot. I'm not sure why I'm crying because America is so far away and I don't want to live there, but it seems that the leader of the free world can't stop killing its best people. I hate communists, but, apart from its wars against communists, it seems Americans should be more afraid of Americans than anyone else. They should be wary of the bloke over the road, down the street, in the next suburb, because he's the one most likely to kill them.

Students are still rioting in the streets and now crowds of Negroes are calling for Black Power. American cities are at war with their citizens. They are not alone. Europe is on fire too and in Germany a violent communist urban guerilla gang led by Andreas Baader and his girlfriend Gudrun Ensslin are blowing up department stores.

Here in Moroki I think of Margaret Baker. She is black. I am white. I don't know her, only just met her, but I want to be with her.

.....

There is another coupling, with another white girl at a dance. She is a visiting sister up at the hospital and we dance all night at another nurses' party. We are both drunk and she drags me back to her room up on the hill behind the hospital. Inside she rips my clothes, grabs the lizard, pulls viciously, no softness, no caressing, just a grab and tug causing me considerable pain. There is no way I am going to yell out because this might be standard practice in expat mating circles and the lizard will just have to get used to it. What do I know? She tries to force herself onto him. Tries to shove him inside her. It seems he might make it. There is a small window, but no, it slams shut, or was never really open, and again he hits a wall. I am sure she knows what she is doing because she is older than me and has an experienced look about her but the drunkenness takes its toll. On both of us. After another frantic bout of pulling and pushing she lets him go, falls flat on her bed and faints. I stand, staggering, watching her until I am sure she isn't dead, just asleep, grab the clothes I am pretty sure are mine, put them on, and walk out into the highland rain. By the time I get back to the bank mess my clothes are soaked and my testicles are screaming. The pain is so bad I have to lie awake until three o'clock before I can settle their nerves. The only way is the traditional way. I take the lizard in my hands, work him hard, but gently, and let him go.

11

Higgs is the ledger examiner and it is his job to close
the doors every day at three in the afternoon and at
midday on a Saturday. As soon as the doors are shut we
all lope back to the bank mess and eat lunch. It is Higgs'
responsibility to close the doors and he does it, every day,
with precision, closing that one first, that one second, as
laid down in the Bank Manual of 1937, just as he does
everything he does, according to a manual somewhere,
including comb his greasy hair. He isn't a bad bloke, but
he irritates everyone in the branch with his pernickety
pickiness, except Watkins and Jenson. They like him.
He makes them look good. Higgs is saving up to buy
a Holden Monaro, with all the extras that can be fitted
before delivery and with a firm plan to fit others when
the car is his. His bank account is awash with money.
He never withdraws. The only entries are deposits. Higgs
rarely socialises with the rest of us. He spends most of
his time in his room, reading motor magazines sent up
from Adelaide, combing his hair and checking his bank
balance. I wonder if he's an Elvis Presley fan, but he
never mentions him and neither do I. We live in a world
without music. I don't sing anymore. Tunes are escaping
me. I try to whistle my favourite Beatles song, 'Nowhere
Man', but the others tell me I am tuneless. I miss The
Beatles, Manfred Mann, Gary Puckett and The Animals.
Where are the Beatles? Have they left India? Have they a
new album out? And I miss the beach. There was a beach
in the capital but after swimming most of the beaches
along the south coast of West Australia from Perth to
Esperance, I had arrived knowing it was impossible for
the planet to offer anything better.

It's another Saturday. Higgs closes the doors. Franky
and I balance. We walk out of the building, happy,

promising ourselves a couple of cold ones from the bank mess beer fridge. Banda Beer is still shit but I'm getting used to it. Drinking it quick helps and sucking it through a mouth full of potato chips.

Franky, I say, tell me more about Wollongong. What kind of a place is it?

It's okay, he says. There are lots of migrants working in the mines and the steelworks.

You ever go up to Sydney?

Nuh. I've got night school during the week and on the weekends I play hockey in the local competition.

I was wondering about that. You don't look like a rugby player and your ears are normal.

Yeah, those animals would kill me. What kind of a town is Genoralup?

It's a shithole full of sleazy Rotarians.

Franky laughs.

Including your dad?

Dad? Nuh. He's not a sleaze, but some of his mates are.

Someone yells at me from the end of the driveway: Jacky! Jacky!

It's Hamish Huxley, local coffee buyer and lunatic driver of a Toyota Land Cruiser. I'd met him down at the Moroki Club over a game of snooker. He was good. One night he set up a challenge.

What about the coffee buyers against the bank johnnies, he said. You poofters up to it?

Poofters? I said. Wasn't it you I saw holding Pete Anderson's dick in the toilets last week, right after he'd taken it out of your arse?

We all knew it was a joke, although not a very good one, and while Huxley wasn't a poofter, we all knew Pete Anderson probably was. Huxley had a mixed race girlfriend of spectacular proportions. I'd seen him with her one night in the lounge bar over at the Highlands Hotel. Huxley was a man I wanted to know. He looked like he had everything.

Huxley is on foot, walking in his heavy-shouldered style, the walk of a rugby player.

Hux, where's the Cruiser?

Down the road. I'm off to Jimmy Irish's for lunch. You wanna come?

Jimmy Irish?

You gotta meet Jimmy Irish. Crazy Irish bastard. You never know what's going to happen with the Irish.

Hang on, I'll get changed out of this stuff.

Bugger that. Come on.

Frank has that warning look on his face again.

See you, Frank.

Jack, he says.

I nod and look back towards the bank mess. Haines stands there, with the ever-ready sneer comfortable on his face. The others have gone inside. Haines looks like a colonial master in his white shirt, white shorts, long white socks and neatly combed hair. Hair is important to Haines, Higgs, Watkins, Jenson, people who have power, or who need to feel powerful. Haines is constantly running a comb through his hair.

Don't save my lunch, Hanno, I yell.

I'll give it to Tarbo, Haines yells. He can chuck it at his wife.

Huxley looks at me.

Friend of yours? he asks.

Nuh, I say. Right, what's this Irish bloke do for a living?

You won't believe it, says Huxley. He's a social worker.

I follow Huxley to his Land Cruiser. In no time at all we are on the other side of town and pulling into a driveway beside a house almost hidden by trees and large shrubs that seem to want to swallow it whole.

Inside is a man who has to be Jimmy Irish, and two others. They are drinking, laughing. The man who has to be Jimmy is Jimmy. He is short, not built like an Irish setter, more like a British bulldog. He is one of those blokes you like, even though, as soon as you spot him, you know he is trouble, but you can't help yourself. Even my mother would like him. I can see him sweet-talking her out of her bedroom after Dad has sent her there with one of his sarcastic comments.

Jimmy Irish scurries over to me and says: So you're the new bank johnny. Heard about you. About time this town had a bank johnny with balls.

One of the other blokes hands me a stubby. We toss the bottles back. Then another one. We're men. It's what we do. After the third they all look at each other, wink, laugh, and Jimmy Irish leaves the room. I can tell something is cooking and it isn't in the kitchen because that's where we are and nothing is on the stove.

What's cooking?

Nothing. Well, something, says Huxley. I told you, you never know what to expect from the Irish. Or the highlands. Up here, my friend, we live our own lives.

They all toss their heads back and I laugh too, without a clue why I am laughing, what I am laughing at, or who. Jimmy is gone about ten minutes and when he comes back his face is flushed and his eyes wink, one after the other. He walks right up to me, takes my arm and leads me to the little portico at the back of his house.

There's a girl in my bedroom, he says. Lovely thing she is. She'd like you to go in there and stick yourself into her.

What?

Oh, yeah. She's not a kid. She's a woman.

My lungs lose oxygen and I gulp air in short bursts. What is Irish saying to me? What did Huxley say he did for a living? A social worker? Are they mocking me? Am I a joke?

Is she a prostitute?

Come on, Johnny, I'm not a bloody pimp. I'm the native welfare officer. Christ Almighty, Mary Mother of Jesus, give me a break.

Jimmy, my name's Jack. Calling me Johnny reminds me I work in the bank and I have to go home and eat lunch with the wankers.

Okay, Jacky boy, what do you say?

You serious?

Yes, I'm as serious as an Irishman could be if you held a blowtorch to his testicles and asked him to kiss yours.

I have no idea what he means but I want to believe him because my testicles are stirring and longing for something they have long longed for, an outcome for their big brother the lizard, a result, but not on the outside; I want in, and something more than a random shot over a sheet wrapping a girl who seems to know as much as I do about the sex business, and if Jimmy really is a social worker or welfare worker then it must be all right whatever it is he is doing.

Jimmy Irish is smiling at me.

What was that all about?

What?

You drifted off there for a minute.

Right. Okay. Jimmy?

Yes.

You know this woman?

Of course. She's a friend. She often drops in here for a cup of tea, or …

What?

She likes you. She saw you arrive. Thinks you're cute.

You're joking.

No, that's why I went in the room, to check, to see if she saw you.

Why is she in the room and not out here?

Jacky, Jacky, Jacky, so many questions. She's shy.

Is this right? How did she get in the house? Did Jimmy whistle to her across the street, call out, she smiles, they talk some pidgin talk, then invite her in?

Jimmy's laugh lines fill his face. You can see he is always laughing. I want it his way, to believe she has seen me, maybe even met me at the bank, is attracted to me, thinks I am cute, wants to be with me. I want to be with her, any her, but this her will do. I am nineteen. My time is passing. I am tired of me, tired of my hand on me, rubbing me, pumping me. I want her to do it for me, a good way, a proper way, with kindness, or even love. Is this her the her? Jimmy is eager. He is the town's native welfare officer. He can't be a pimp. He is an official working for the territory's administrator. He knows everyone. What I am about to do is not against the law. There is no law that says white and black must not enter each other, cannot marry, cannot live in the same house in the same street, not like in America's Deep South, or South Africa. Here we are free to be in whoever will let us in. Jimmy is a man of the world and he will have heard about Martin Luther King who was surely fighting for this very right. Maybe met him. Jimmy is bringing us together, white and black. Perhaps this is part of his job.

Okay, I say.

I can feel my pants expand so rapidly I think they will split. This is it. She will be the first. I will wake up tomorrow and know what has happened because I am sober. Whatever it is that should happen when a man enters a woman, will happen, now, for me. Yes. Am I up for it? Am I ready?

I open the door, look in. The room is small. There are two single beds and I can see the girl sitting up on one with her knees up. My mouth dries up. I search for moisture. Not a drop. The blinds are closed but I see her smile. She looks young, not that young, but young enough for me to know she isn't an old maid. Her teeth are white. She has nice teeth. My mother would like that she has nice teeth. The rest of her is as dark or darker than the room. I smile. I jump. Jimmy is behind me and whispering in my ear, Her name is Mary. Then he is gone. She lifts her dress. I drop my pants, climb onto the bed and shove my entire manliness towards her, lizard first, the rest following and we strike a wall of flesh. The girl shifts, takes me in one hand and moves me into an opening that seems to suck me in, and it is as though I remember it even though I have never experienced it before. This is what I have longed for, the soft moist welcoming. My brain disappears and my body takes over and does the job I had no idea it knew how to do, the moving in and out, the breathing, the building, the urgency, the sudden final thrusts. Everything shudders, shakes, explodes and fills me with a new and wondrous happiness. My brain returns, regains focus and I feel a great relief that it is done, that it has finally happened, that I have entered a woman and she has received me and been nice, gentle and giving, and I have reached a conclusion that clearly pleases my straining testicles. I smile, she smiles, says something in her language, or the local creole, or pidgin, Hungarian, Latvian, I have no idea, or just makes a noise. I pull my pants back on over my dripping, still throbbing, still thrusting penis.

Thank you, Mary, I say.

Masta, she says.

When I turn into the lounge room they are all waiting for me and Jimmy jumps off the settee and laughs.

Well? he asks.

Yeah.

You want to go again?

What?

Jacky, my boy, you can go as often as you can go.

He walks me to the bedroom door, out of hearing of the others.

Your first, right? he asks.

No, no, there were a couple of girls in the bank, back home.

Better than a wank, aye?

My face fills with red. I turn quickly and enter the bedroom. The girl is exactly where I left her.

Masta, she says.

Just for a second, I think I am in love. Then I remember Margaret Baker and I know I'm not and that what I am doing makes me more unworthy and if Margaret has any sense she will stay well clear of me because even I can feel my filth. I know what I am about to do is not illegal, but is it moral? Is it right? But I can't escape the joy of the lost virginity, cracked, never to be regained. Not once, or twice, but three times, because I have to go in again. She is there, each time, on the bed, waiting, expecting, and before she leaves the house Jimmy goes back in the room and at the door he puts a hand in a pocket and pulls out some notes. I see this, then reject it, not wanting to know it is true. No, she likes me. She saw me arrive, she thinks I'm cute, she wants to marry me, have my children. Is she the woman I left Perth to find who will lead me into a world where she belongs to an ancient and honourable family, and when I return home triumphant she will show my father what kind of man I am? No, not this woman on the bed, she's not the princess, Margaret Baker is, but until Margaret Baker comes to terms with her destiny and her royalty and we begin our lives together, I have to become a man, a complete man, a man who can please a woman.

What a day: my virginity lost to Mary, a sweet young woman who allowed me in, helped me, welcomed me. I no longer need the Islands of Love. I am in the Town of Love. All I did was walk into a room, smile, and a woman lifted her skirt. No looking around, walking around, no box of chocolates, no expensive hotel room, no tight squeeze in the back of a Volkswagen. And no questions asked, just a smile and we're in. There is only one thing left to do, get pissed, it is the only way to celebrate, to prolong the euphoria of the loss. I drink hard, fast, mouthful after mouthful of potato chips, and the harder and faster I drink and eat the happier I get and I go back again to the bedroom but Mary is not there and the others laugh at me when I walk into the kitchen and I laugh with them at my confusion but who cares because I am oh so happy.

Jimmy, you got any more beer? I ask.

Jimmy laughs. We all laugh. I run from the room, stumble out to the back garden in the rain, and throw my guts.

There's no more beer, yells Jimmy from the back door. This party has no beer. You got any cash?

I wipe myself on my bank whites. Find some notes in a pocket, stumble back to Jimmy, hand him whatever it is I have in my hand, someone gets in a Land Cruiser, drives off in a muddy spray, and returns in no time with more beer and potato chips and beer nuts. The drinking starts all over again and I drink until all memory is obliterated and I wake up on Jimmy's floor with convulsions underway. I get up and run for the garden where I chuck chips and nuts and whatever is left until the green slimy bile appears and even then I keep chucking until there is nothing left to chuck but air and the memory of the loss. I don't chuck that, not that memory, that is mine, forever. I am sick with drink and stupid food but I am happy, happier than Larry and I say out loud: Fuck you, Dad, now I'm a man. You see that? Did you? Stand back and let me through.

12

A letter arrives from home. And a newspaper. The letters don't interest me anymore. Their contents mean nothing to me, cannot compare to my new life of sexual maturity, of man knowingness. Thomas, my older brother, is doing well in the law firm and will soon complete his articles, whatever that means. Billy is, of course, also doing well, in both schoolwork and sport. Dad's business continues to grow and he recently went on a fishing trip with a number of very important businessmen, including a barrister. Woopty doo. Everyone is always doing well. We hope you too, Jack, are doing well. Yes, Mum, I am a statement machine operator in a bank branch run by two incompetent idiots and a man with a Holden fetish. I am also an incompetent idiot and that's why they gave me a girl's job. I get pissed every night and have begun to fuck myself stupid. I have one clear rule when fucking: no white girls. No offence, Mum, but they don't seem to get it. With the black girls there's no opening the car door, or buying chocolates, or courting period, or even flirting or foreplay, you just call out, they cross the road and you stick yourself right in. Cool, hey? When I come home I am going to move down to the other end of town and shack up with an Aboriginal woman. There's no law against it.

I look at the piece of paper. I disgust myself. I tear it into little pieces.

In little Genoralup nothing changes, nothing happens, things are still the way they were and are and have been and everyone does well, but outside, in places beyond, there's a madness brewing. Students are protesting in the US over the Vietnam War, one of the long-haired radicals in Europe, someone they called Rudi the Red, is shot but not killed, Canada has a new prime minister, a French-

Canadian, and French students nearly topple the big man with the big nose, Charles de Gaulle.

13

I keep going back to Jimmy Irish's, looking for her, for Mary, my first, wanting her again and again. Jimmy is never home. Mary never walks by when I sit on his veranda. I want more free love. Should I march in the street, storm a building, burn a bus? One night, Jimmy is home.

Jimmy, I say, where's Mary?

Who? he says.

Mary, you know, that woman I had sex with.

Shit, Jacky, I don't know. I never saw her again.

.....

I am sitting at the Beast when Margaret Baker walks in and stands at the enquiry counter. Smiling. Waiting. Is she waiting for me? I don't give myself time to answer, rise quickly, perhaps too quickly and almost run to the counter.

Margaret, I say.

Oh, she says. I met you up at the nurses' quarters.

Yes. Nice of you to remember.

She smiles. The lizard shifts.

How long have you been in Moroki? she says.

Not long. I came up from the capital. I'm from Perth.

There was a girl in my school from Perth, Jennifer Gunning.

Are you serious? What school was that?

Pymble Ladies' College.

Oh yeah, all the Gunning girls got sent east. Perth's PLC wasn't good enough for them. I went to her sister's coming-out party last year. They live in Peppermint Grove in a massive house.

That's unbelievable, Margaret says.

I think Margaret Baker is thinking she might like me. I warn myself. Remind myself I am too dirty for Princess Margaret, that I am no Lord Snowdon. But now she is in front of me, the dream comes alive.

Where did you go to school? she says.

Grammar, I say.

I've heard it's the best in the West.

Ha ha, yeah.

What are you doing here?

Well, I'm supposed to be at uni doing law, but, you know, the examiners and I didn't see eye to eye.

Margaret Baker laughs. Mr Jenson's door opens.

Right, Miss Baker, I say quickly, how can I help you?

She nods politely and offers an enquiry that I can answer easily, speedily, but I don't, I take it nice and slow, with great deliberation, as though the future of planet earth is at stake. And when she leaves the building I return to the Beast and kick her as hard as I can without breaking a toe.

Easy, boy, says Franky. You planning on making out with Margaret Baker?

You know her? I ask.

No, but I heard rumours.

What kind of rumours?

That she's some kind of genius, that her father's a legend and that if he finds anyone mucking around with her he'll shoot the sod.

Haines walks past our machines.

You're a fucking loser, Muir, he says.

Maybe, I say, but not at table tennis.

Haines is showing signs of moving on from not liking me to detesting me. I remember the look, have seen it before, on the faces of the bully boys in school. I can't keep my mouth shut.

Hey, Haines, you wank with the same hand you play

table tennis? That might be your problem.

Haines gives me the look. I snort.

Jack, says Frank, take it easy on him. Don't push him too far.

14

Huxley and his mates have a plan.

What we do, he says, is get a truckful of old tractor tubes, drive like the devil out to the Gulani River, chuck the tubes in, jump in the tubes, and go like a singing hyena down the rapids.

You blokes are insane, I say.

Maybe, but, fuck me, what fun it is.

Right, so you're down one end of a stack of rapids and your truck's up the other end, how the fuck do you get back?

That's where Felicity comes in.

Who's Felicity?

You haven't met Felicity yet?

Nuh.

Then you haven't seen the finest pair of pins this side of anything. What about Howard Merkel, you met him yet?

Nuh. Heard of him. He's another mad bastard coffee buyer isn't he?

Yeah, and he's my cousin.

.....

Huxley meets me at the bank, same time as the previous Saturday, right after closing. This time he gives me enough time to run upstairs, change out of my whites and into t-shirt and shorts. Then I climb into his truck and he plants his foot, tears out of the bank driveway and heads for the higher hills like a bat out of an oven.

Shit, Hux, I say, could you give a bloke time to settle his nuts on a seat.

Your nuts are going to be so hard and numb after

today you won't know whether you're sitting on balls or brazils.

Huxley laughs so hard it is clear he thinks this might be the funniest thing he ever said. I don't want to change the mood but there's a question I have to ask.

Hux, do you know Margaret Baker?

His face is a new colour and the lines on it shift from a laughing position to something more serious, almost angry.

You all right? I ask.

Yeah, he says.

She's not your girlfriend is she?

Shit no. What's going on with you and her?

Nothing. I met her at a party.

Jacky boy, you're not playing with her are you? Because if you are you're looking at a gun up your arse. Her dad protects her like Fort Knox.

No. We just met. Once. I know she's out of my league.

You bet your arse she is. Blokes like you and me, we should stick to the whores. Margaret is the Madonna.

What?

You never hear of that, the Madonna–whore complex?

Nuh. I know about the Madonna and I know what a whore is.

Jacky: one you fuck and one you love. A mate of mine I went to school with down south told me about it. He's studying psychology and he said that Freudian bloke thought it all up. Now, in your case, can you pick which is which? I'll give you a clue, the one you fucked up at Jimmy's, she's a whore.

Right. And the Madonna is the one you marry?

Yeah, but neither of us is going to marry Margaret Baker. Look, us long-term expats have it pretty good up here but we have to recognise that certain things and certain people are off limits. Jim Baker is an old-fashioned bloke and a legend on both sides of the fence. He went through all the right rituals, paid a bride price, the lot, then married Margaret's mother in a church before they had any children and if he says don't fuck with my daughter, we don't. You with me?

Yeah, I say.

Huxley drives down roads and up tracks and I lose all sense of where we are, where we have come from and where we are going. The bush seems to grow as we drive, becoming thicker and thicker, more impenetrable, mysterious. It's not like the light-green bush back home. This bush is deep-green and thick with vegetation and something else, something hidden. Every so often a native appears out of the heavy green growth and stands, sometimes stares, sometimes waves, but always with penetrating eyes, as though determined to let us know something, perhaps not to come too close because there is something back there, behind him and he belongs to it and if we venture too far in it will take us, eat us, limb by limb as we scream and beg for our lives.

The bush thins. Relief. I can see through it now. Then the trees dwindle and part and open out into a sort of beach, not a sandy beach, but one full of rocks and pebbles and Toyota Land Cruisers.

As we pull in I see a magnificent creature move across the pebble beach. She is tall, athletic, with perfectly formed calves, and legs that go all the way up to her arse and what an arse. I have never seen anything like it. From her arse up her curved midriff to her straight and strong shoulders there is no part of her that is not the work of a supernatural being. Human nature, I decide, is not capable of creating such beauty. Two people fucking like animals could never produce such a creature. She is an angel, a goddess. Surely a Madonna. She turns around, slowly, her hair drifts with the movement, and I wait with quickening breath for her face which should be nothing less than the face of a princess – but it is, a lot less, but not so much less that it takes away the joy of beholding the rest of her.

Shame about the face, says Huxley.

What? I say.

You were dreaming, weren't you, you filthy bastard?

Well, even Jesus would weep. She dazzles.

Yes, and she's taken.

That's a shame.

We climb down from the truck and walk over to a small group working on rubber tubes.

Hey, Flicka, yells Huxley, you gorgeous, edible slice of woman, come and meet Jack, a bank johnny. He's just spoofed his pants over you.

Felicity turns, opens her mouth and even though it issues a stream of obscenities it is still not quite enough to lessen the look of her majestic form. I feel the hot red rush up my face, the red of tomato, strawberry, cherry, all the reds available and then a deeper red, almost beetroot.

Jesus, says Felicity, can't you keep your dick out of your mouth, Hux?

Everyone laughs. Not just because of what she says but because of the way she says it. She has an English accent, one of those odd, funny, regional accents, not one you hear regularly on the television, or in the movies, but one often made fun of by English comedians. Then one huge hand raises itself in a wave, the hand of a man, a hand that does not belong with the rest of her body, but there it is, alongside another one, two man hands on the ends of her magnificent arms. Maybe she's a mix, mainly woman, but with the mouth and hands of a man, evolved to survive in this tropical madness. She is clearly no Madonna, nor a whore, somewhere in-between. I must ask Huxley if there is an in-between.

106

My face lightens and cools as the blood slowly flows back through my veins and arteries. I'm not sure about all the godlessness. The expats are exciting to be with, much more exciting than the bank johnnies, but they seem to have lost all inhibitions, manners, and that quality my mother said we must never lose, decorum. Their mouths open to let loose all kinds of shock and horror, but, I keep saying to myself, I'm no longer a virgin because of these people, they have made me a man of the world and because of their gift to me, I will cope with their obscenities. It's all new, the language, the fucking, everything, but what a place to learn.

Right, Jack, says Hux, this is one fuck you have to meet. Howard Merkel.

A man walks towards me, sort of. At first he almost seems to be walking in another direction, then he changes tack and heads crab-like towards us. He holds out his hand. I take it. He takes mine. He shakes it, but doesn't quite look me in the eye, sort of peers out from under his forehead. He is a handsome man, built like the man they called the hooker I watched in Rugby League games back in the capital. He is about my height, solid, and he has a cat-like look about him, like he is ready to pounce, to dive into something, anything, like he is forever poised for some kind of action. Interesting mix, the crab and the cat, both solitary animals, both darters, both dangerous.

Gidday, says Merkel. You're a bank johnny?

Yeah, I say, gives me the shits too.

There are about ten of us, including Huxley, Merkel, Felicity and her boyfriend, Tom Exeter. There are more tubes to offload, makeshift rafts to assemble and, of course, beer to drink. By the time we hit the water we are half-cut.

We enter the water from the small beach and don't have to do much because, although the water seems peaceful enough, it soon reveals its powerful current and rips us along at a rapid pace, twisting and turning and running between high walls of rock and overhanging foliage. I concentrate on the river and don't look into the undergrowth. I am on a large tractor tube and in no time at all facing rapids.

Shit, I yell.

Keep your arse in the tube, yells Exeter, but not too low or you'll bruise the bejesus out of it.

My arse is too low. I drop about ten feet down a rapid and a rock smashes my arse into a thousand cuts and bruises. From then on I ride the long low rapids like a seasoned rider and take the short and sharp falls poised to protect my bleeding, pulpy bum. All the way down the mountain stream we laugh at and insult each other. During a brief lull in speed, along a small stretch, Tom Exeter comes up alongside me.

Are you the bank johnny who has the hots for Margaret Baker? he asks.

What?

Word travels fast up here.

No hots. Just asking about her.

Mate, don't fuck with her.

I nod. I'm getting the message. Margaret Baker is sacred, not to be touched, not to be joked about. She is the Madonna. Unless, of course, you are Jesus, well not Jesus, that would be incest. Joseph, you'd have to be a Joseph, to be pure, to be worthy. A bank johnny is unworthy, what's more, I have made it clear I am open to a casual, off-the-street fuck and that makes me filthy-unworthy, although no one says that. Exeter hasn't said that. But he has obviously heard about me, will know of me and my visit to Jimmy's. Is Exeter a casual off-the-street fucker? No, he's got Felicity. And he doesn't look like one. His hair is neat, his back straight, his clothing ironed and orderly. So who will get Margaret Baker, who will win her affections? Who will her old man choose for her? Who can be worthy? Prince Charles? A Kennedy?

Jacky, look out, screams Exeter.

Too late. I tip over a short sharp drop and lose my ride. Exeter passes me and gathers my runaway tube.

You all right?

Yeah.

......

At the end of the run Felicity is waiting for us with the truck. She has offloaded all the eskies and is walking around in a bikini designed for Ursula Andress. She looks better in it than Ursula Andress. Except for the hands. And the face. We need Felicity because Ursula Andress does not have offloading esky hands. We drink all the beer, Felicity drives us back where we started, takes her legs and her man, Exeter, and leaves. Huxley says he has to go too, but it will help if I go with someone else because he is going home in a different direction.

Merkel says: You wanna come with me? I'll take you back to town a different route.

Huxley laughs.

And when he says a different route, says Huxley, that's what he means.

Merkel is another lunatic driver and I am barely in his Land Cruiser before it is off and charging up a track I haven't noticed until we are on it and ripping it to pieces.

No point in taking a track if you can't rearrange it, yells Merkel.

My arse is on fire. I shift, trying to find a way to sit that doesn't include pain. I can't find one.

You got a bruised arse? asks Merkel.

Yes, I say. I think I took a couple of rocks up it.

He laughs and says nothing more for a while, as though concentrating on his driving, as though determined to get us home safe and sound and in one piece.

You and Huxley are cousins? I ask.

Yeah, he says. We did time together at Shore. We got to hang out with Australia's future business and political leaders. That's what they told us at school anyway.

He doesn't say anything again for a while. I look out the window. We're in the jungle. What's in there? Then the road opens out and two girls are in the middle of it staring at us, not moving, not waving, just standing, as though the road is theirs and we have no right to be on it. Merkel hits the brakes and skids up to them. They look frightened now. Merkel jumps out of the Cruiser and chats non-stop in pidgin. He goes so fast I have no idea what he is saying. Then he walks over to my window.

You up for it? he asks.

What?

Come on, puss puss. You know, a fuck.

Shit. You can't just drive up to a chick in the middle of nowhere and ask for a fuck.

Jesus, Mr Bank Johnny, you got a way to go. I thought they said you were a gin jockey.

He has a look in his eyes I haven't seen before, not on anyone I have ever known. It's a strange mix of fun and a kind of dark madness but it is not enough to stop me, to make me pause and think of any other possibility because I have to be up for it. It is the only way I am getting it, by being ready for it when it is offered. Somewhere deep inside I am offended by this mad-eyed man leaning in the Cruiser window, disgusted, repulsed, but I am also excited and thrilled by the danger.

Listen, Jacky, says Merkel, this is how these people live. A casual fuck is nothing to them. They do it all the time with their friends, their neighbours, their cousins.

It's a way of life, long before we arrived. We're not asking them to do something radical.

What about Margaret Baker? Where does she fit?

Ease up, Jacky boy, Jim Baker's daughter doesn't fit the mould and if Jim Baker says don't fuck with my daughter, I don't.

His eyes are laughing.

Come on, Howie, I say, would that stop you?

Fuck no, but she's not my type. These two are. You in or out?

Right. I'm in.

Good boy. I'll set it up.

He walks back to the girls, speaks again in rapid pidgin, turns, gets back in the Cruiser and speeds off.

Where are we going? I ask.

Up the road a bit, says Merkel. They said there's a clearing. We're going to meet them there.

Why aren't they with us?

They didn't want to get in the truck in case someone saw them.

Why would that matter? You said we weren't asking them to do anything radical.

No answer. I don't question him again. He doesn't look like he'd like any more questions. The girls were right: there is a clearing. Merkel parks the truck and gets out.

You wait here, he says. I'll have a look around.

I wait. I'm nervous. I'm not sure. In town it seems fine, but out here, who knows. We're surrounded by a kind of bush not known to me. It's not like the tall grey timber of Genoralup, peppered with zamia palms, banksia trees and melaleucas. This is not my place. It's not Merkel's place. You drive down a road out here and you have no idea what's up ahead. Could be anything, anybody. Up at Jimmy's it was different, everyone seemed to know the game, but driving along a road in the bush and meeting two village girls, asking if they want to fuck, and then fucking them, that doesn't fit. And where are we going to do it? In the back of the truck? On the grass? What if someone else drives along the road? What then?

Merkel bursts out of the bush, running hard. He's at the driver's door, yelling, screaming, and behind him are two men with clubs and what looks like a spear. He opens his door and slams it in one fluid movement as the spear flies, glances off the back panel and Merkel laughs and races the Cruiser screaming and charging down the road. I am shit-scared but Merkel is chuckling, yelling and cursing. He drives like the lunatic he is right up to the Jungle Bar. We get out. Go in. Get pissed. Drive up to Jimmy Irish's. Wait. A couple of girls walk along the street. We whistle. They come over, walk into the house, lift their skirts, we enter, Merkel hands them something, they leave, we get pissed. At three o'clock in the morning I get up to chuck my guts.

15

I have been back to Jimmy Irish's house more than once. Mary has not been back, but there have been others. I am losing count. But I want more now, there's something missing and I think it might be conversation, someone I can talk to, relate to, a girlfriend. Someone black. She has to be black. The white girls confuse me. They flirt. They tease. Not the black, well, Dorothy Sogata teases me at the enquiry counter, but it's different. Would it be the same back home? Would I want to be with an Aboriginal girl? There was one, once, a tall, elegant Aboriginal woman I thought was Indian. I watched her at parties. She always looked so sad, so angry, yet worldly, experienced, way too much for me, the little virgin boy from the bush. All I ever did was watch her. One night at a party, someone found her in a bathroom, lying in the bath, with her wrists slashed. Jesus, I cried, I should have said something, let her know that I thought she was beautiful. I didn't go to her funeral. None of my friends did.

Although they were there first, in Australia, they are a minority. Up here, the whites are, and because we are few in number it makes it all so much easier, and so much more dangerous.

.....

Dorothy Sogata and I talk in the bank and what once seemed good fun is now frowned upon by Watkins, the accountant, and Jenson, the manager.

One day Watkins says: Jack, we understand you and Dorothy Sogata are getting along very well. She is a lovely young woman, but we all have our place up here in the highlands and ours is not the same as theirs. We are here to do a job. You are here to do a job. We don't want a scandal. Remember, we have our place, and they have theirs.

I want to say: You're a fucking racist, Watkins.

But I say nothing. I nod. And then, I'm not sure how it happens, if it is because Watkins has warned me off, or because I am genuinely falling for her, it's on, me and Dorothy. Does it start one day because of the way she looks at me, or because she whispers in my ear as I walk past her in the street? Or because I am no longer a virgin, but ready, a man of seed and confidence? Now I am in Dorothy's little house, where she lives alone, and I am naked, she is naked and we are rolling through her three rooms, and bouncing on her bed and off her bed and she is showing me things I have not known, had not dreamt about and she never makes fun of me or says I am young and inexperienced, she helps me, goes with me, takes me, caresses me, shakes me, tosses me, and oh, she is strong, but she never lets me kiss her. I forgive her that, because of everything else. I can live without a kiss, but I can no longer live without the rest, all that Dorothy is teaching me. She builds in me a fire for learning.

I am in Dorothy's house every night, but when she comes to the bank we greet each other in a normal, formal manner, except for our eyes, they climb into each other and say things like: Tonight? Yes, tonight you will enter me with a leap that will take you into the deepest bit of me and I will hold you there and work you with my inner juice and bounce you from the ceiling. I am in love with Dorothy, with her muscular, athletic body, with her smile, her courage, her willingness to ignore the colonial racist pigs who want to keep us apart.

16

My paper arrives. The students are still revolting in Britain, Europe and America. And the Beatles have formed Apple, their own record company. I live in a town without music. Every so often we go to a house where there are records and a record player, but that's rare. For the rest, no music. Not one bank johnny has a guitar, or if he does, he keeps it well hidden in his room and only plays when we are all dead in sleep. Polly Farmer's new football team, West Perth, is looking like a winner. He's the first Aboriginal to coach a league football team and I'll bet he's giving the shits to a few of the old-timers. I wonder if Polly has a young sister and whether she's tall, elegant, athletic, like Polly, and if she's a Madonna or a whore. Here's another question: If I was back home, in Australia, in a town like Pingelly, would I sit out the front of someone's house and whistle at a couple of Nyungar girls across the street? And if I did, would they go away and come back with their brothers and beat the shit out of me? I must ask Dorothy if she has any brothers.

.....

One night the bank johnnies all get pissed with a coffee buyer who owns a truck and when the Jungle Bar closes we decide to visit Watkins' house and invite him out for a drink. Just for a laugh.

I walk up to the front door of his neat little bungalow with Paterson and Franky. I knock, and Watkins opens the door and says: Muir. What do you think you are doing?

Me and the boys, Wato, I say, thought you might like to come and have a drink with us on our truck-bar.

Muir, you're drunk.

Of course, sir, that's why I'm about to say I love you, Wato, and I want to have your children and why I'm slurring and finding it hard to stand upright or even see you properly. That is you isn't it, Wato, you old prick? Can I come in and lie down for a day or two?

Go home, Muir.

Someone is pulling my shirt. I think they want me to stop, but I can't.

Not until you come and have a drink with us, I say, because we're all here, Prem, Franky, and over there another truckful. We're a truck full. Get it, ha ha, a truckful of blokes, a truck full. You bought us a drink once and now we want to return the favour, take you out for a night on the town, show you what goes on after dark. In the dark. Ha ha.

There is movement behind him. His wife pushes him aside. Watkins stands behind her.

Who do you think you are? she asks.

I am the Ghost Who Walks, I say, Mr Walker, The Phantom.

If you do not leave now, I will call the police.

Someone takes hold of my arm. I shake it free.

Please, Mrs Wato, madam, we were just passing on our truck-pub and we wanted your old fart here to join us for a drink. You might like to join us too. You are most welcome, my dear.

She looks at me and I think I understand why Watkins has a need to direct us with such certainty at work. It's because he is directed with such certainty at home.

Go away, she says. Now! Or I call the police.

Just before I go, Mrs Wato, are you aware that your husband is a racist?

She moves so fast I don't see the door move and as soon as the slamming is complete I hear Watkins say from

116

the other side of it: Muir, you have three minutes to leave or I'll call the police.

Right, you racist, I yell. I'll leave, but if you talk to me again about talking to native girls on the enquiry counter I'll call the fucking United Nations. You got that?

This is too much, Mrs Watkins yells. I'm calling the police.

I turn to dash for the truck. Prem and Franky are already there and on the back of the truck. I fall over and shout: Wato's whatsit is calling the fucking police. Mayday mayday.

The truck is on its way by the time I get to it and I have to jump. I don't quite make it but two blokes grab my arms and pull me on board. We have just enough beer left to do the job properly, to get well and truly pissed. I think about visiting Dorothy, but my brain collapses and I fall asleep.

.....

It's Monday. We're all back at work. Mrs Watkins usually visits on Monday, but she doesn't. Watkins doesn't mention our visit. I reckon it is because he knows he is a racist and he doesn't want me saying it out loud. He doesn't look at me. I look around the office. No one is looking at Watkins. All have their heads down and their bums up. Even Higgs, but his is always down and up and then I realise not everyone was on the truck. Higgs was in his room with his head in a Holden HK manual his father had sent him.

17

A mob of us are up at Jimmy's place. Two new blokes turn up. One runs a family coffee plantation and the other bloke is a kiap, or patrol officer. Phillip Curtin is the plantation owner. He's a wiry little man who dresses like a fashion model. He looks odd up here in the highlands, in his waistcoat, tight-fitting shirt and tailor-made jacket and pants. Mike Hogarth, the kiap, is a big bloke with rugby shoulders. He not only has big wide shoulders, he has a big wide mouth that lets the world in and then out again with a huge roar that shakes the neighbours' house and sends its occupants running outside thinking there is another earthquake on the build. Earthquakes are not common, but earth tremors are and they always send the locals scampering for fear of the gods of the earth rising up and kidnapping small children and beautiful young women, taking them into their caves, molesting them and sending them back up as soiled goods. Sometimes you see sad dishevelled looking natives and the word is that these people have been below, abused, and sent back.

Last week, I say to the group, I saw a woman with no face.

She'd be one of the faceless, says Huxley.

What's going on there?

Some of the natives sleep too close to their fires, says Hogarth. Then roll into the coals late at night. I've seen it more than once out on patrol, a person whose face has melted in a fire.

We had a chap teaching us maths at school with a face like that, says Curtin. But his skin wasn't that smooth. Looked like his mother might have dropped him face first in a frying pan.

Curtin is an interesting mix of sophisticated expatriate and dedicated islander. He tells me his family took advantage of a project after World War II to populate the island with experienced farmers and old soldiers. His father was both an old soldier and an experienced farmer. They once farmed out west in New South Wales but when their land gave up all it had, the family walked.

If we got the rain down there we get up here, we'd still be there, I can tell you, says Curtin.

I don't ask him what school he went to, but my guess is Scots College or Shore.

Jimmy is getting pissed. We are all getting pissed. Some people need a reason, a cause to celebrate. We don't. We never do. We get pissed because that's what we do. Then we fuck.

Right, says Jimmy, let's have a party. Hux, why don't you go get that nurse you've been hanging out with. Phil, don't worry, we'll find you someone, and Jacko, what about Dorothy?

What? I say.

I am stunned. How does he know? I haven't told anyone. No one knows. Not even Franky. I sneak around to Dorothy late at night and creep out early in the morning. I blush.

Come on, says Jimmy, this is a small town, Jacko. You can't go shagging a local without the rest of us finding out.

Jesus. Who knows then?

Just us, the overlappers.

The what?

The overlappers. You got the white expat racists over there. The black nationalist racists over here. Then in the middle you've got us, the people who don't give a fuck what your colour is, what your religion is, where you come from, what school you went to, how much money you've got. Us. That's you and me and Hux and Phil and Dorothy and some others you haven't met yet. Black and white and all in together.

And Merkel, I add.

Well, yes, although Merkel is in a league of his own.

What about Mike?

I look at Mike Hogarth.

Not me, he says. I'm married, I'm a kiap, as good as a cop up here and it's not a good look for me to be seen fucking around. But you blokes go ahead.

Yeah, says Huxley, that's what he says, but when he's out on patrol, who knows where his dick will end up.

We all laugh.

And I'm a good mate of the future prime minister, George Kanluna, Hogarth says.

He might be PM material, says Huxley, but he's an islander through and through and he's not shy when it comes to dipping the wick.

Hogarth leaves us and we all squeeze into Jimmy's four-wheel drive, picking up girls from the hospital native nurses' quarters, from this house and that house, and Dorothy's house.

Dorothy, you home, I yell.

Jacky, she says. What do you say? What do you want?

You want to come to a party?

A party? Are you mad. You will get into trouble.

No, it's with the overlappers.

What overlappers?

Jimmy Irish, Hamish Huxley, Phil Curtin.

Okay, those men. I like those men. I am coming. Wait.

I am so happy, a party with my girlfriend, a native girl, a party full of other men with their native girlfriends. This is the life. This is where I want to live, up high in the mountains in the Town of Love.

Dorothy and I leave the party early. She doesn't drink. She doesn't like it when I go around to her place drunk.

Why you come here drunk, Jacky, she says. You don't love me?

Of course I do, I say, although I never say that I love her, I only ever say, of course, or respond in some other way. I can't say, I love you, Dorothy. I'm not sure. What I do know is that I like fucking her and she likes fucking me and I like her strength, her willingness, her eagerness. Dorothy and I fuck ourselves stupid most nights and I begin to keep count, the number of times I enter her and achieve orgasm. One night at the Jungle Bar I tell Merkel.

I hold the world record at six fucks, he says, all in one night, cumming each time. You have to cum. Every time. A fuck without a cum is not counted a fuck. See if you can beat that, Jacko boyo.

I nod acceptance, but I say nothing. It doesn't seem seemly. And I say nothing to Curtin, Jimmy, Franky, anyone, not even Dorothy. Least of all Dorothy. I don't think she will join in the competition and I want her to, I need her to. I win. I get to eight. Now I tell everyone, well, Merkel, Jimmy, all the coffee buyers. They call me Jacky Big Fuck.

Look, it's Jacky Big Fuck, they yell across the street.

I blush and write home to Mum: Hey, guess what, I have finally won an important competition. I am now the champion fucker up here in the highlands. Oh yes, I beat all the local champs and now hold the record for the number of fucks with cums in one night. You proud of me, Mum? Please tell Dad, I know he will be. Makes me laugh, all those students you read about in the paper protesting about sexual freedom, all they have to do is come up here. I burn the letter.

That night I dream I'm flying again, but I can't come down because there's a mob of men chasing me and every time I try to land they attack me with clubs and long knives. Eventually I get so tired I have to land but I land too close to a cliff and the men chase me off the edge. I have no energy left to fly and I wake up in a blind panic.

18

Dorothy is funny, cheeky, naked, but after that there is not much to Dorothy. I try to engage her in conversations about what she wants out of life, the future of the islands, independence, about her family. She is not interested. I want to talk to her about her religious beliefs, her Christianity, but she swears she has none, even though she attends church every Sunday. She says she does it for her father.

Your father? I ask.

Yes, she says. My father is a big man.

What does he do, the big man?

He is a police captain.

Oh. Where?

Not far from here. In the next district.

Does he know about us?

If he knows, he will not like.

Why not?

He is a proud man, and my tribe is a proud tribe.

It's true, there are racists on both sides. He is a black man and he wants his daughter to hang out with black men. On the other side, the white bastards in the bank want me to hang out with white women, or no women. Dorothy and I are overlappers and I'm a gin jockey.

You know they call me a gin jockey, I say.

No, what does it mean? says Dorothy.

It means I have sex with gins, black women. So what do they call you?

They call me Dorothy. We have no word for this. Black women have sex with black men and white men.

Dear Mum, I write, my black girlfriend is the daughter of a police captain and if he finds out we are fucking he will kill me.

I flush the letter down the toilet.

·····

I am on the little path that leads to Dorothy's house. I see movement in the bushes. There is something there. I know there is. Oh, Jesus, not the thing, the haunting thing, the thing I think is there but I know it can't be, can it? No, not here in the village. I am safe here. Stupid boy, there is no such thing. It's just someone on the move. I think no more of it, because locals are always on the move, delivering parcels, collecting bags of stuff, visiting friends, family. I have no idea why they are forever moving, but they are. I am almost at her house when a man in a police uniform emerges from the bush and stands in front of me. Was it him in there, following me?

He looks like he has a job to do. His truncheon is out of its holster, in his hand, and swinging.

Yes, I say.

You, he says.

There is movement again, either side of me. More police. More truncheons.

Not this way, he says.

Why not? What's going on?

No. No.

He begins swinging his truncheon in an arc. I turn slowly, no sign of panic. Stay calm. I walk back the way I came, towards town. He follows. I quicken my pace. He increases his. I run. He runs. I am confident I can outrun him because I have always been a good runner and he is wearing police boots. Then I hear more than two feet running after me. I don't look back. Someone enters the path on my left and a truncheon or a lump of wood strikes my shoulder. It hurts. It doesn't stop me. Another blow catches my right ear. It makes an ugly sound and I think I might have lost my ear lobe. I run harder and thank my legs for their speed and their willingness and all those years of high school athletics. I keep running until I no longer hear feet behind me and my lungs gasp, then I stop and put my hand to my ear and it comes away with blood. My left shoulder hurts. All I can think is that Dorothy's police captain father has heard, has taken action, has sent his men to beat the shit out of the white boy and that he's a racist bastard, wants me gone, or dead, or at least maimed and maybe my lizard removed and shoved down my throat because although he is a police captain and a man of some education he is still a savage and brutal beast.

I lie on the ground. I have no idea where I am. Because I don't wear a watch I have no idea how much time passes. My shoulder hurts, my ear bleeds, but it was worth it all to have that brief affair with Dorothy Sogata. I also know that Dorothy and I are finished, that I will never see her again, except in the bank. I don't, not for three weeks. She stays away. She knows. Her dad's boys have been to her as well, or dad has. Then she walks in and I don't get up. I send Franky to the counter, pleading a toilet break. By then my ear is almost back to normal, but it will carry the scar forever. My left shoulder still hurts. I am left-handed and that side of my body is taking a beating in the islands. First the Volkswagen over the cliff in the capital, then the police attack.

When I come back from the toilet, Franky asks: So, you and Dorothy?

What do you mean, me and Dorothy?

Come on, Jack.

I can see he knows.

Who else knows?

Don't know, but Haines has made some comments.

Fuck Haines. Anyway, it's over, Frank. Done. Dusted. Finished.

Was it her father?

Fuck, Franky, you knew about him?

Yes.

Why didn't you say?

Well, I wasn't really sure about you and Dorothy, until now. Don't worry, there's plenty of fish in the sea.

Thanks, Frank, that's a big fucking help. How many more have police captain fathers who beat the shit out of white boy lovers?

Arr, that's how you got your ear and shoulder. It wasn't a game of rugby up at Curtin's place after all.

Frank, you and me, right, no one else. Or we're both dead.

Mum's the word, he says. And, Jack, I'm no racist, but you might be walking a fine line here. This isn't our country, it's theirs and one day soon they will be taking over completely.

19

When my paper arrives I get on a plane and fly to Algiers and free the Israelis hijacked by a gang of Palestinian terrorists. It's a plane full of women and children and I don't understand why people would do that to a mob of Jews who have surely suffered enough because it was only twenty-five years ago that Hitler and the other inhabitants of his lunatic asylum tried to wipe the lot of them off the face of the earth. Israel is where Jews are from. It's where they all should be, not roaming the world getting the shit beaten out of them by mobs who hate them. That's what just happened to me. Do I look Jewish? Of course not and I don't fly to Algiers but it's the kind of big meaningful battle I'd like in my life, which is a bit sad, ratshit, and stuck in a bank. I miss Dorothy. I miss the sex, the bouncing off walls sex, the running around a house naked and laughing sex. I miss the sense of manliness sex brings and I fear going back to the boyishness of wanking. It's the only way most of the bank johnnies are getting sex, by taking their lizards in their own hands. Especially Haines. If he's not pumping iron, he's pumping his dick.

Haines has bought himself some dumbbells and each day he goes into the spare room downstairs and lifts and lifts and you can see in the way he walks after one week that he is sure his body is already taking on a new shape, more and more like the world's greatest body, Charles Atlas. Walk is not the word, strut is closer. Not only does he look like a masta in his white whites, he is now building a body to go with his sense of himself.

.....

It's my turn to do the week's menu, to go to the markets with Tarbo. He's built like a brick barbecue, square and not far off the ground. I like the bloke. Something solid about him. Okay, he beats his wife, but he lets her get a few punches in and he doesn't kick her when she's down and every so often he lets her beat the shit out of him. It's a marriage of equals; the violence not all one-way. We don't talk as we walk to the markets. His English is not that good and my pidgin is almost non-existent. I have no idea why we do this. Is it to remind him that we are in charge? Maybe to give us some interest in our highland lives, to stop from going completely troppo? Higgs made a big fuss the week he was on, preparing a new menu, buying all the vegetables while Tarbo walked alongside carrying the bundles, but the rest of the blokes just go along for the walk. I take the menu from last week and nod at Tarbo.

Same pella dis week, I say, thinking I am picking up the lingo.

Tarbo giggles.

The markets are packed with people, pushing, arguing, loading and unloading. There are almost as many sellers as there are buyers. Now I know what some of the movement is about, that endless two-way flow on the street. Tarbo picks up potatoes, sweet potatoes, tomatoes, looks at a great range of produce that I have never seen before and buys piles of leafy stuff that looks familiar.

Just as we are ready to leave I see Margaret Baker. Then she sees me. She hurries towards me.

Jack Muir, she says.

Hello, Margaret Baker, I say. What are you doing here?

When I'm home I buy all the food for our household.

So do I.

She smiles.

No you don't, she says. It must be your turn to do the menu.

Caught red-handed, I say. And I'm not doing anything

anyway. Tarbo's got it all sorted.

She looks at my ear that still carries the mark of a truncheon-wielding policeman.

A few of us were mucking about, I say, you know, bit of a rugby game.

I can feel the red blood rush above my shoulders. I look at the surrounding produce for something salty.

Better go. Great to see you, I say.

I almost run and then have to turn back because I realise Tarbo is still in the throng, somewhere. Margaret is watching me.

Sorry, Margaret, I add, I'm under a bit of pressure at work. I haven't balanced yet.

I think the Madonna believes me. It doesn't make me feel good. That night we eat pork chops, sweet potato, potato, and a mess of greens Tarbo bought while I wasn't looking. That night I dream I am at a party. I see Margaret Baker across the room. I walk towards her, but when I get to where she was she is no longer there. It doesn't matter how many times I walk through the crowd, I never find her.

·····

After Dorothy and I split up I go a bit more often up to Jimmy Irish's and wait around for someone to walk by. Merkel has gone south for a few weeks and I kind of miss him, his daring, his madness. Then May walks into the bank. I am talking to Higgs about a transaction I have put through the day before when Franky gets up and goes to her at the counter. She is shy and barely lifts her head as she speaks to him. When he gets back to his machine I say: Who was that, Franky?

Easy, Jacky boy, he says. She's new. Works over at the Lutheran Church School. I think you're out of luck.

Why's that? I ask.

She's Lutheran, get it? It's a German version of Christianity. Strict. They probably shoot sinners.

She's beautiful, Franky.

They're all beautiful to you, Jack. Find yourself a white nurse. This one's another Margaret Baker, you better forget her.

I can't. She is beautiful, in a black Julie Christie sort of way, with strong features, broad lips, a nice run of muscle down her arm and eyes that suggest something you know you will never know. She doesn't look like the other native girls. Her face is the sweetest face I have ever seen. Her skin soft and creamy, like melted dark chocolate and her breasts are as I like them, barely noticeable. She doesn't come in for a week, but when she does I am ready. She doesn't say much but I do and I make her smile. The pressure on a new relationship, I realise, always makes me nervous and getting to know May takes a lot out of me. On week three I find out where she lives and suggest I might drop in for a cup of tea. She drops her head, of course, but smiles, maybe she blushes, and probably thinks I never will, probably thinks I am just another white man making silly jokes, but I am serious all right and before I know it and before she knows it I am knocking on her door, inside her house, inside her, most nights of the week and, yes, I fall in love with May. At least, I think that's what happens, because while the relationship is developing my nervousness increases and I drink even more than usual. May isn't like Dorothy, she doesn't seem to mind if I arrive drunk and her father isn't a policeman. And sex with May isn't as bouncy, in fact there is no bounce, just quiet, gentle movements. Is one lust and the other love?

20

The bank mess is a moving feast. Blokes come and go. I spend so little time in it that I don't notice some blokes arrive and then I do and then they go. Some are transferred to other islands, to the capital, or other towns on the main island. Others move back south to the safety and security of their hometowns with their fringe-dwelling black communities that are well away from the hustle and bustle of mainstream white activity, while the odd one or two under twenty-one returns home and finds himself in another uniform, back in a building full of men, then off to Vietnam to fight the Viet Cong.

William Foley is different. I notice him as soon as he arrives. He's a bit darker than your average Aussie, his mum is probably Italian or Greek. He's not very good at table tennis but he has a go and one night after I've thrashed him again we sit out on the balcony in front of my room and knock back a couple of beers.

Newcastle? I ask.

Yeah, he says.

What's it like?

A shithole. As shitty as this beer you blokes drink. But they've got a great soccer team and I play in it. Even made a state team.

Soccer? You've probably heard of Sir Stanley Matthews then?

The wizard of dribble. The magician. If I can keep playing as long as him I'll be stoked. How come you know about him?

Mum and Dad used to give us *The Boy's Own Annuals* when we were kids. They were English and full of soccer stories.

Hang on, they called it football, right, 'cause all we

use is the foot. Not like Aussie Rules. That should be called handball.

In WA we've got this great player, bloke called Polly Farmer, who's had a massive influence on the game. Now there's even more handball.

Polly Farmer?

Yeah. Abo bloke.

Foley frowns. Not much, but enough to make me think I might have said something he didn't like.

What's up?

You said an Abo bloke, like it was amazing an Abo bloke could do something special.

I didn't mean it like that. He's a footy hero of mine. Just about all my footy heroes are Abos. Polly Farmer, Irwin Lewis, Sydney Jackson, Lionel Rose.

Lionel Rose? Yeah, right.

I reckon he would have been great. Make a nippy little rover.

Did you see any of the fight, the one against Fighting Harada in Japan?

Nuh. You?

Yeah, it was brilliant. And every Abo stood a little taller that day.

You reckon it's okay to call them Abos?

It is for me.

Why's that?

Because I'm one of them and if you and I keep on getting on, you can call me one too.

You serious? You're Aboriginal?

Yeah.

Bugger.

Foley laughs.

What's it like being an Abo?

Fuck off. What's it like being a white bastard?

Same, huh?

Because I don't look Abo, most people think I'm Italian, or Greek.

That's what I thought. You don't ever tell them?

Why the fuck would I? So then they can call me a coon, a boong, a tarbrush, and give me the shits for no reason? You won't tell the others, will you?

Tell 'em what?

That I'm a coon.

I wouldn't tell 'em I'm a white man.

I like Foley. Why don't I know Abos like him back home? The locals in Genoralup are about his colouring, but they look like Abos, talk like Abos, walk like Abos. Or do they? May doesn't walk like Dorothy. The Genoralup Abos are a good mob. They play footy and have jobs and there's no reservation, not even a separate bar for them at the Freemason's Hotel. They have reserves in towns like Gnowangerup and Katanning and separate bars in the local hotels. You drive through those places and you can smell the hate, the fear, the racism.

Foles, I say, are there any good Aboriginal soccer players?

There's a bloke called Charlie Perkins. You might have heard about him.

Nuh.

You remember the Freedom Ride? Mob of people got on a bus and drove through New South Wales and protested against discrimination. One of the places they went to, Moree, had banned Abos from swimming in the local pool for over forty years. Racist bastards.

I remember that, I say. I thought they were communists.

That's what the government wanted people to think, but they were smart. Charlie Perkins was the first Aborigine in university.

No he wasn't, that was Irwin Lewis, he was the first

and I know for sure because he went to my old school.

Did he finish?

Shit, I don't know.

Right, Charlie was the first to graduate then. Got a Bachelor of Arts. I've seen the photo of him in the poofter gear.

We laugh.

He wasn't one though, says Foley. Bloody good bloke. I know one of his cousins.

21

May greets me at the door. She looks like she has been waiting for me. She doesn't look like the highland girls, she looks more Polynesian, from Hawaii, or Fiji or somewhere even more exotic. I don't speak, just grab her arm and pull her towards her little bedroom. She laughs. I laugh. I remove my clothes and help her take hers from her exquisite body. She lies on the bed and I roll on top of her, go quickly to her place of entry, find my way in, and move, gently, because May is a gentle woman full of what seems to be love and kindness. I have no time for foreplay, for seduction, and May doesn't seem interested either. My confidence is growing. If, on the odd occasion, the lizard cannot find a way in, I make a quick adjustment and seek a more suitable location. When my final rush is over and we both lie still I ask her if she would like a cup of tea. She says yes and gets up to make it.

.....

I am reading *The Carpetbaggers*, another Harold Robbins tome. There's a bloke in it I like, Nevada Smith. He's part Kiowa, an American Indian tribe from Oklahoma. He's strong, tough, a killer, a lover, a man. His parents are killed by some bandits and he chases them down one by one and kills them all like the racist dogs they are and begins a life of crime, killing and sex. Along the way he is insulted and abused for being Indian, mistaken for a white man, all kinds of women throw themselves at him and he becomes a movie star. He has piercing blue eyes. I try to make mine pierce and I dream of important battles to fight and incidents to avenge. If only some evil prick would oblige and kill May and force me to track him down like the pig he is so I can slit the bastard's throat with my hunting knife and avenge not only May but all women like her who have been ravaged by men like him.

.....

I don't knock, not anymore, I just walk in. May is sitting at her little kitchen table in her tiny kitchen. She smiles. I smile. When May smiles you lose control over your face. I look towards the tiny bedroom off the kitchen. It is the only other room. She smiles again. She gets up from her chair and puts her empty cup on the sink.

Can I go to the toilet first, Jack? she asks.

No, May, I say, no toilet.

We know it's a joke. Of course she can go to the toilet. She knows she can, but she can see the eagerness in my eyes, the hunger in my body. May knows I have come for sex.

When she is done and I am done and we lie naked on her bed I say: May, you are a Lutheran, right?

Yes, Jack.

What do Lutherans have to say about sex?

She turns away.

I mean, do they say that you shouldn't be doing it, that it is a sacred act and that you should be married first?

Is it what you believe, Jack?

I laugh, then May laughs and I push myself into her again.

We are still. I sit up and look at her silky naked blackness. She has the perfect figure, a thirty-five, twenty-three, thirty-five, the Tania Verstak numbers, those belonging to the former Miss Australia and Miss International, the first foreign-born Australian to win a beauty pageant and the only famous woman my dad ever seemed to get sweaty over. Tania Verstak is out of my range, but May is mine.

Have you heard of George Kanluna? I ask.
Of course, May says. He is a big man.
How big?
He might be our prime minister. Have you met him?
No, but I keep hearing about him.

22

In the bank my work seems to be deteriorating. If not for Frank's support I would be in Watkins' office every second day.

Frank leans over me.

Jack, he says.

Yes, Frank.

You see that form there, on top of the stack?

Yes.

That's a deposit.

Funny man.

So why did you just enter it as a withdrawal?

Oh shit. Did I?

Yes. Do you think you could do me a favour, just a small one.

Sure. What is it?

Just balance one day a week. That would be a big help.

He's right. I've lost concentration. All day I think of May and Margaret, the one I have and the one I want. The whore and the Madonna, no, she's not, May, she's not a whore, but Margaret is a Madonna.

Watkins is standing over me.

Yes, I say.

My office, Muir, says Watkins. If you wouldn't mind.

I follow him, imitating his angular gait. I see Bill Foley suppress a laugh. Haines sneers.

Watkins sits and I remain standing.

Your work is deteriorating, Muir.

Is that so, I say.

Yes. It might then be timely to remind you that you already occupy one of the lowest positions in the bank and that the only other low position is already occupied.

Is that so.

I know you think you are funny, Muir, but funny

doesn't help you maintain a position in The Colonial Bank of Australia, Australia's first and finest bank.

Is that ... all you have to say, Mr Watkins?

Know that you have been warned, Muir.

Thank you, sir. I appreciate the warning.

I lie. What I really want to do is drag the racist bastard outside in the street, remove all his clothes, tie him to a tree, douse him with honey and wait for the ants. I don't. After dark I go to May's house.

When I get home I sleep in short stints. Something is wrong with my dreaming. I can fly but have great difficulty maintaining direction. I wake up from two dreams after I crash into trees. I turn my light on and read until it's time to get up for work.

.....

I am in Byrne Brothers buying a pair of underpants. There is not a great range but when it comes to underpants, I'm practical. I look for Bonds. I can't find them. There's another brand. I am thinking about buying them when I look up and see May. She is looking at me.

May, I yell, hello.

She smiles and turns her head.

I walk up to her.

May, what are you buying?

I want to put my arms around her and if kissing was what we did I would kiss her, but it isn't so I don't. I still want to. Outside, in the light of the day and in the big open spaces of Byrne Brothers shopping market, she looks great. Her perfect figure is not disguised by her simple dress. Her hands are soft and feminine and I take one in my hand. She pulls it away.

Jack, not here, she says.

But, May.

No.

When I get back to the bank I realise I forgot to buy underpants.

.....

Haines is a piece of shit. His mouth rests in a permanent sneer and nasty stuff comes out of it. Watkins is a racist prick. All the bank johnnies are shits. Except Foley and Franky. And Prem. But the rest, all shits. Why are they shits? Because they shit me. All right maybe not pure shits, like Haines, but sometimes they are so close I can't tell the difference and sometimes they are so far from Haines that I almost want to tell them about the life I am living alongside them but I never do because they are boring and their lives are lived around the Jungle Bar, the Moroki Club, or the bank mess where their faces are often stuck in car manuals, bank statements or letters from home. Franky is okay. When I arrived he knew stuff I didn't but now I seem to know more than him, about sex, at least. The bank johnnies aren't really living here, just saving money for that car, that house, maybe a horse, a plane, who knows, but whatever it is it's back in Australia. They don't mix with the locals, the whites or blacks. If a local doesn't have a bank account with us, they don't exist.

I look across at Franky. His machine seems bigger than ever.

Franky, I say.

Yes, Jack. What can I do for you?

How long are we going to live like this?

I don't know about you, Jacky boy, but I've only got three months to go and then I'm out of here.

Bastard!

I look down at May. She looks up at me.

May.

Yes, Jack.

You're beautiful.

She laughs.

Your breasts are perfect, I say. They fit your body nicely. Your legs are strong and have well formed calves. Your waist is delightful, your arms have muscles, but it is your eyes that reveal your soul.

May shakes her head.

May, I want you to marry me. Marry me, May.

We both laugh.

I'm serious.

No, Jack. You must not marry me.

I love you, May.

She turns her face away. Then back.

Jack, you must marry a missas.

A what?

A missas, a white woman.

I roll on my side. She thinks I should marry a white woman? All this lovemaking, for what? For nothing, meaningless, just a romp in her single bed in her little shack on the side of the hill, right next door to the Lutheran Church. She thinks I should return to my own kind, my skin group, and she to hers. I have a lump in me, a thing that has been growing ever since I arrived in the highlands, it feels like a huge potato and it is lodged in my chest. My body heats up, my face fills with red. I look at my pink, freckly, blotchy skin. I hate it. I hate my kind, my race, my family. I hate Australia. And I hate myself. Not for the first time, but this time it isn't about sin, or Jesus and God, or the others, the bullies, the teachers, the parents, the older brother, this time is about me, the me I have become, the only me I know but a me that I am sure is not the real me. The me I have become is a drunken, random fucking machine that fucks anything that moves and it is the way it is because of my white colonial skin, my pink blotchiness. May allows me in because she pities me. Or can she see the other me, the real me, the me in pain, the sick and demented me that seems to have lost his way, or never found a way? Maybe I'm going troppo. They say it happens up here. The lump in my chest wants to break out and splash its pus on anything near it, poison it, drown it in its thick, sick, yellowness.

My body shakes and takes quick shallow breaths. I can't let May see me cry. I roll back on top of her and thrust my lips at hers, but they never meet. May too has never let me kiss her, never let my lips touch hers, let my tongue in her mouth, our faces have never met full on, pressed into each other, sucked each other. May has only ever allowed cheek to cheek facial contact.

May doesn't have any salt in her little house. She has sugar and tea and a bowl of fruit and vegetables I haven't learnt the names of yet.

I bury my face in her exquisite shoulder and push my lizard into her.

Oh, May.

She lets me in and I push as hard and as far as I can in an effort to reach a point too far, so far in returning will be impossible, but once inside her loveliness my sad and filthy whore fucking body finds new strength, new life, and begins moves it has learnt well. It doesn't take long, it never does, and when it all arrives in one sudden burst and keeps on arriving I keep on thrusting and laugh and cry and push my face into the pillow so May can't see it.

When I am done the lump seems smaller.

23

Higgs walks up to me with a letter. I open it. It is an invitation to attend Margaret Baker's eighteenth birthday party, with a friend. Why me? Doesn't she know I have been warned? Of course not. I should take May, that would keep her away from me. But I can't. I love May, but May will never be my equal, she has said as much. If we married she would always live in my shadow, like Mum lives in Dad's shadow, like Dame Pattie Menzies in the shadow of Sir Robert, Australia's longest-serving prime minister. Maybe my love is like the love of a colonialist for his subjects, his wards, his property. I don't want that. I want an equal, someone I can share my life with, someone to talk to, about anything and everything, about the existence or otherwise of Jesus and the big man, God, about communism, colonialism and capitalism. And I want a Madonna. May isn't quite a Madonna, or a whore, she's somewhere in between. Maybe more of a whore than a Madonna. If she had held out, resisted, not let me in so quick, not in her house, or in her body, that might have made a difference.

Margaret's party is not for May. Margaret is smart, educated, and her party will be full of well educated and sophisticated people, black, white and in-between.

I go alone. Margaret greets me on the veranda with a peck on one cheek. My arms rise instinctively, to hold her, embrace her, but I force them to alter course, my hands to grasp her biceps, squeeze them a little, and my mouth to say: Margaret, thank you for inviting me.

Good of you to come, she says. I know you must be busy, what with maintaining the bank mess kitchen, and balancing all the books.

I smile and allow my lips to brush her cheek. Does

she blush? I think I do, but I am saved because another guest arrives.

I go easy on the drink. The party is full of the town's elite, including the two Byrne brothers, Huxley, Exeter, some very impressive looking native girls and boys, no doubt those who have done time in expensive private schools down south. Hogarth is there too, with his wife, a plain looking woman who barely looks at me when we are introduced. Word is he went to Geelong Grammar's Timbertop with Prince Charles. It seems everyone is there but the bank johnnies and Jimmy Irish. And Merkel, I don't see Merkel.

Hogarth sidles up to me.

You see that Byrne brother, he says, the big one?

Yeah.

He killed a Marakin.

A what?

One of the Marakin people, a bloke who worked for him. Hit him with a baseball bat because he said he insulted him. Smashed his skull.

Shit. What happened?

Nothing. All hushed up.

How come you know about it?

Mate of mine was a patrol officer in that district. Everyone knows about it. No one says anything. I think he'll be leaving though, when independence comes.

Hogarth laughs. I'm not sure why he's laughing, but I attempt to join him with a small chuckle.

How come he's here?

He's a Byrne brother, son of the big man, Arthur Byrne. Right now everyone needs him on their side. And you see that bloke, that's George Kanluna.

I look where Hogarth is pointing. I see a man with his back to us.

I can't see him, I say, but I'm hearing about him.

A big man, George, and getting bigger.

Hogarth goes back to his wife. I don't think she approves of me. Her eyes say: Don't come near me, you filthy little man.

I understand, but I need to talk to someone, or just stand next to them and not look like a rat in a nursery. I see Exeter standing alone.

Can I buy you a drink? I ask.

He punches me on the arm.

Where's Felicity?

Not feeling too well, he says. She's got a tropical ulcer on her leg and the doc thinks she might have malaria.

Tom, no, not one of those legs?

Yeah, I'm not happy. Anyway, she doesn't like these sort of things much. She thinks they are full of stuck-up snobs.

What about you?

It's part of my job to stay in touch with important people. I'm finance manager for Byrne Brothers up in the highlands and at something like this you are going to meet a lot of people who are making decisions, or who will be making decisions in the future. And I like free piss.

A waiter walks past.

Better grab another one, says Exeter, before the speeches start.

There is a speech by old Jim Baker, Margaret's father. He speaks well, of his pride, his hopes for the future and of the love and pride he is sure his deceased wife would feel on such a day. We all sing happy birthday. I have a word with myself because I am drinking faster than I intended. I go for a walk in the extensive, well planned and well attended garden. I take a path that winds its way through tropical plants, including banana trees.

I hear a noise behind me. Is it that thing that keeps following me? Shut up, Jack, there's no thing. And it isn't,

144

it's the opposite of the thing. Margaret Baker. She has found me. I don't know how. Did she watch me leave and follow? I don't ask. I am full of joy. We sit on the grass at the edge of the garden.

What will you do when you leave here, Jack? she asks.

What makes you think I'm leaving?

You people always leave.

She has a look in her eyes. I look away so she can't see the look in mine.

I wish I knew, Margaret. My older brother is a lawyer. I could go into my father's business, but one thing's for sure, I won't last in the bank.

She laughs. I watch her laugh and want to hear it again.

I am the only boy from my year at my old school who works in a bank. My parents are ashamed of me.

Shut up, Jack, I say without a sound. Don't overdo it. She doesn't have to lose respect for you. I'm nervous. I fidget. I want vodka, salt, salty vodka. I look at her. She's beautiful.

Are you religious, Margaret?

Not really. We were brought up Methodist, but that was more about Mum than Dad and he hasn't pushed it since she passed away. What about you?

Used to be. Sometimes I still talk to Jesus. Not sure why. I liked him, preferred him to his father who seemed to be some sort of big, angry bloke who insisted on killing people who didn't agree with him.

She laughs again.

Have you thought of studying philosophy? she asks. It won't help you get a job but you seem to have a natural bent.

Margaret Baker thinks I have a brain? The Madonna thinks I have a brain?

Then something unexpected happens. She leans in

towards me, I turn and she kisses me full on the lips. I close my eyes but can still see her dancer's neck, the soft black skin and I know the rest of her even without seeing it naked, the small but wondrous breasts, the slim tight waist, the eager thighs, the running legs and the feet of an angel. When I reach her feet the slow kiss lingers even longer and the messages to my brain are of such variety that I'm trembling and confused and among them is a sense of almost love that I want to last even though my heart pounds with a need to escape and my nerves jangle because they know that if anyone sees us they won't bother to call on God to wipe me clean, they will do the job themselves.

Margaret, I say.

Don't you like me, Jack Muir?

I do Margaret Baker, I like you too much.

There is a sound behind us. I know it's not my imagination because Margaret hears it too and we both get up quick and walk back to the party, our hands brushing in their swing. Huxley is waiting for me. Or did he arrive just ahead of me?

Jack, he says.

Hux.

You want a lift home?

He knows. I can tell. He wants me out of here.

Okay.

When we get to his Land Cruiser he turns to me and says: If I ever see you in the vicinity of Margaret Baker …

What's a vicinity, Hux? Can I say hello? Can I walk the same side of a street, use the same public facilities, buy an ice-cream in the same shop? This isn't Deep South America, you know.

I don't see it coming. I am not ready for it. His fist slams into my ribs. My wind leaves me. I have no wind. I have no fight. I drop.

I'm sorry, Jack, he says. She's too good for you, for me, even Tom Exeter. You got it, Jack? There's a line here.

I mumble, cough, stay down. Should I roll over and stick my feet in the air? Huxley walks away.

24

Another day slaving over the Beast and I think I'll go mad.
I look over at Higgs. His face is deep in paper. I look up
at the front door and in walks Dorothy Sogata. She sees
me as soon as she enters. She probably pauses a second
at the door, aims her face in my direction, then pushes it
open, ready to hit me right in the eye. She almost smiles,
then turns quickly away. Sometimes I miss Dorothy, her
mad crazy body bouncing me off the bed and around the
room, but I don't miss her father's angry black men.

Dorothy doesn't go direct to the teller's box. She sidles
up to the enquiry counter and William Foley gets out of
his chair at the back of the office and walks over to her.
Well well well, it doesn't take her long to find another lover
and he's the newest boy in town. Part of me wants to warn
him. Part of me wants him to cop a beating when he tries
to enter her house. And part of me is relieved because it
means Dorothy might stop eyeing me and smirking at me
and looking offended and hurt as though I am the only
white man she has ever been with and I know for a fact
this is not true and that most fathers of young women her
age are not controlling racists and don't mind that their
daughters sleep around because collectively the locals are
somewhat more promiscuous than we are. But then the
joke would be on Dorothy, because Foley isn't really a
white man, he's a black man.

Dorothy leaves with a parting look over her shoulder
in my direction. I wonder if it is all for my benefit. Foley
heads for the toilet. I follow.

How's Dorothy? I ask.

He jumps.

Shit, he says. You came up quick.

You and Dorothy, you doing it?

Fuck me, Jack, what is this?

She used to be my girlfriend.

Oh. You're done, right?

Yeah.

She's hot. You're not jealous?

Nuh, we're well done and dusted.

Hey, Jack, if you're a gin jockey and I'm the son of gin jockeys am I a gin jockey's gin jockey?

We both laugh.

Jack, what the fuck are we doing in a bank?

.....

Some stuff baffles me. Like France getting the bomb. It's on the radio news and in the paper that comes from home. Charles de Gaulle has exploded a hydrogen bomb. Great, now all the big countries can kill everything. And democracy is starting to confuse me. At the Chicago Democratic Convention students and hippies riot, cops charge, and people are maimed and killed. And the English cricket tour of South Africa is cancelled, all because South Africa refuses to admit Basil D'Oliveira. D'Oliveira, according to the paper, is not a black man, but a coloured man. In South Africa they go by shades and I wonder if he is a similar colour to Margaret Baker and, if he is, then the officials keeping him out must be demented racist arseholes.

25

When work is done for the day, I look at Franky, he looks at me, we balance, I throw my arms out as though we might hug, we don't, we shake hands, he says he's going to visit his nurse, I kick the Beast in the guts and head over to the Jungle Bar for thirty or forty quick drinks before the usual evening meal. I don't make it, the meal. Howie Merkel turns up out of the impending dark and fading blue, or the mountains, the mists of grime, wherever it is he has been hiding. As soon as he enters the bar the noise level seems to drop. People turn, see who it is, take a deep breath and go back to their conversations, their drinks, their inner thoughts and fears.

Hey, says Howie.

How're they hanging, Howie, I say.

He leans into me.

They're hanging all right, hanging out for a beer, or fifty, some sweet pussy to suck and maybe a punch in the face from some dumb shit willing to have a go.

Once I tried to repeat what Merkel said and it didn't work, got no laughs. There is something demented about Merkel, but when he says the nasty shit he says, right there in front of you, you have to laugh because of the way he says it, the mix of his lilting poetic tones and the cheeky charming face that he puts on to go with it.

I can see trouble up ahead. I am ready for it. I want it. I have missed it.

We drink for a couple of hours then head down to the Moroki Club and drink more. We try to start a game of snooker but the tables are booked solid and even though we are sure we put our names on the board they aren't there when we go to complain to the bastards who seem to be involved in every game. Merkel offers to take them on, all four of them, outside, now, anytime, but all they do is laugh. We eat something. No idea what. Then we go up to Jimmy Irish's but he isn't home so we drink a bottle of Bundaberg Rum on his back step. When it's empty Merkel pisses in it, puts the cap back on and puts it on his Land Cruiser running board.

What's that for? I ask.

Next party I go to and see one of those snooker thieves, says Merkel, I'm swapping their rum bottle. That'll teach the maggots to fuck with me.

Merkel chuckles a strange, deep chuckle. I haven't heard him chuckle before. It makes me think of my grandfather's old outboard motor, the Seagull, the one on the back of his ancient dingy.

Jacky boy, says Merkel, what about we drive over to May's and she can get one of her friends in for a four-way fuck.

Howie, that's not May.

Whaddya mean that's not May?

We're not doing that.

Mate, don't you go fallin' in love with her. These people are great for fucking but …

I stand up and stumble away from the step.

Have you stuck one up her arse yet, he yells. They love it up there. She's probably had her brother up there.

I go to his Land Cruiser, grab the bottle of Bundaberg piss and hurl it at a tree. It misses, falls and smashes on a rock.

Get fucked, Merkel.

I stumble over to the tree, pick up the broken bottle neck and hand it to Merkel.

And stick this up your own arse.

Jacky. Jacky. I was joking. I know she's your girlfriend. She's a lovely lady. And I wish you all the best for your future happiness. The Lutherans would love to have you in their fuck, sorry, their flock.

Howie Merkel laughs his other laugh, the one that turns a mood around, even after he has said the nastiest, most insulting thing. He hasn't changed my mood but he keeps trying. He stands up and joins me pissing into the shrubs beside the house.

Nothing like a good piss in the wind, right? Jacky? I was joking, mate, fuck me, I'd never fuck May. She's all yours.

I'm buggered, Howie. Think I'll go home.

What? Back to that fucking bank mess, with all those poofs? You must be joking.

He turns. He hasn't finished. He sprays me.

You're a piece of shit, Howie.

Maybe, Jacky boy, but let's go find some sweet pussy.

We don't find any. Merkel drives around like he does, with wild abandon, paying no attention to intersections. We hear a siren. There's a police truck behind us. The cops in the truck are led by an old mate of Merkel's, Pete Silvester.

What the fuck are you blokes up to? says Silvester.

Nothing that you'd be interested in, says Merkel.

Well get off the fucking road before I take you home and let my wife work you over.

Fuck me, Sil. Not that. Anything but that.

Silvester's wife is a strong, athletic woman and a legend in the town because she punched an ex-expat in the face after he grabbed her arse at a party. Knocked him flat for ten minutes. When he came to he was lying on the front lawn with a busted nose and no pride. He left the island soon after.

Okay, says Merkel. We're going. I'll take this deadshit home.

You pissed? says Silvester.

What's it to you?

Nothing. Just asking.

That's the way it always ends. Sil asks Merkel if he's pissed. Merkel says what's it to you and Sil replies, nothing, just asking. They both laugh so hard their heads look like they are falling off then Merkel drives away and Silvester goes back to patrolling roads without cars.

Merkel doesn't take me home because he sees a couple of maries on the side of the road that he likes the look of and after a brief conversation in pidgin they get in the back of the truck and we head back to Jimmy Irish's.

How we going to get in, Merkel?

Who gives a fuck. I want a fuck. We'll bust a window.

When Merkel is in one of his fucking moods, nothing stands in his way. If Jimmy can't be home when we want him home, fuck him, we'll make his home our home. And we do. Merkel busts a side window, climbs in and lets us in the back door. He doesn't turn on a light, just grabs one of the girls and heads for a bedroom. There are only two. I head for the other one, the one where I had my first. The bed is made and I pull back the sheets.

You like? I ask the girl.

She smiles. She is sweet. She climbs on the bed. I remove my clothes, she lifts her dress and the lizard finds his way into her. He shoves himself into her. Again and again. They are always ready these girls, the girls off the street. They lift their dresses, open their legs, and in we go, smooth, moist and easy. It's over quick. Always is. As soon as I sit back Merkel is at the door.

Come on, swap, he yells.

What?

Yeah. She's ready.

Who?

Mine.

What's her name?

Mary. What's yours?

I turn to the girl and say: Jack. Name belong me.

Martha, she says.

Merkel laughs: Martha? He pulls me off the bed and launches himself at Martha.

When we are done, rather, when Merkel is done, we take the girls down the road a bit and they get out of the back of the Land Cruiser and walk away.

You all right, asks Merkel?

Yes, I say.

But I'm not. I feel sick. I am licking my arm. It's salty. I am angry. I'm not sure why I'm angry, or what it's about, or what to do with it, but it reminds me of something that I can't remember but I wish I could because then I could do something to ease the rush of burning blood. The lump is there again, the one in my chest. There's another lump, or thing, something, somewhere outside, in the jungle, following me, ready to pounce, fuck me up the arse, eat my face, do something to finish my miserable life.

Merkel drives like an idiot and I don't care. I am rather hoping he might miss a turn and plough into a tree, or a fence, a house, anything that will cause us to slam through the windscreen and smash our heads on something that will kill us, instantly, at least maim us until this time, this mood, passes, or until the Phantom or Jesus or some other prick who's supposed to be looking after us turns up and tells us what it's all about. I feel like smashing Merkel but I don't have the energy, the desire, or a good enough reason. I have lost my way, my moral core, my reason for being. Jesus is dead. The Phantom is a comic book hero. My dad thinks I'm useless. My mum thinks I've been poisoned. Margaret Baker is denied me.

We're here, Merkel says.

Where? I ask.

Where you live, you stupid fuck. The bank mess.

Oh.

Hey, what say we shake up the bank johnnies.

What you got in mind?

I don't know.

No, think I'll go to bed. I'm fucked.

Jesus, Jacky, you're a fucking pooper.

I get out, quickly, before I can change my mind, but when I get to the front door, it's locked.

Fuck!

What?

The bastards have locked me out.

Right. That fucking does it.

What?

We'll climb the railing.

Merkel drives his Cruiser up under the veranda, close to one of the pillars. He gets out and climbs up onto the veranda. I join him, surprised I still have the monkey in me. Once there we climb through my window and then Merkel has the fire-extinguisher in his hands and I know I am in trouble, but the anger is still with me and the hot blood and enough energy to grab it from him and burst into Haines' room yelling: Fire! Fire!

Haines jumps out of bed but not quick enough and I catch him full in the chest, then I turn away and run into the next room and blast the bed, the walls and the body lying under sheets. Outside I hear a voice yell and run out to see Merkel with the other extinguisher in his hands and blasting three blokes cowering before him, including my best mate in the building, Franky Fletcher.

Shit, Franky, I yell. Sorry, mate. We'll fuck off. We're pissed. I'll clean it up.

Christ Almighty, Muir, yells Franky, and then other voices join his.

Fuck you, Muir.

You fucking wanker, Muir.

Fuck off you gin-jockeying arseholes.

That must have been Haines. No snort, so he didn't think it was funny. He can't resist a gin-jockeying crack. He must be getting lonely, just him, his hands, and his dumbbells. Merkel is screaming as we run down the stairs, out into the yard, into his Cruiser and away, but too quick to maintain control and the Cruiser slams into the bank manager's portico, the one outside his office where he takes his smoko, his morning and afternoon tea, demolishes it, collapses it in a nice, neat pile.

Fuck, Howie, you've got me fucking done for.

Merkel laughs and laughs.

You were done for, Jacko, long before you met me.

Howie.

Yeah.

Take me around to May's.

It's late, but May lets me in, as always. It doesn't matter how late I am or how drunk I am, May takes me in. She is a Christian and maybe she sees something in me, something I can't. She has been sleeping. At the door she peers out towards Merkel's Cruiser. I push her through the door and inside.

Who is that, Jack?

Howard Merkel.

Him a bad man, Jack.

I know, May. I'm sorry.

I stumble to her bedroom and fall on her bed. May does not join me. I hear her fussing around in the kitchen of her tiny house.

May.

Yes, Jack.

Come to bed, please.

Jack, you don't want sex, please.

No, I just want you to hold me. Say something to me. Tell me I am not a bad man, even if you think I am.

May walks into the room and sits on the end of her bed.

Jack, you not a bad man. You treat me good.

May, I'm tired.

Go to sleep, Jack.

But I want sleep too much. Sometimes I want a big sleep.

I drift off. I'm running in a jungle. Something is chasing me. The thing? It has to be. It must be. I run and jump in the air, trying to fly. The thing is almost at me. I can smell it. I can feel its breath on my arse. Not my arse, please, don't eat my arse. I jump higher. Then I fly. I don't look down. I can't believe I'm flying.

May wakes me early with a cup of tea.

Jack, I have no blood, she says.

I think I know what she is saying, but I don't want her to repeat it.

Jack, you hear me?

I say nothing.

Maybe I be pregnant.

I look at her. I love her. She is sweet and kind and beautiful, but I am not ready to be a father, not like this, this filthy dirty piece of shit, this is not a fathering man, this empty shell, this useless maggot. I have a long way to go to be like my father, a solid man, a man with position, status, and a man to respect.

What do we do, May?

I have some gin and I go to a friend for a hot bath. This sometimes works. Jack, you must leave, now, before the neighbours wake up and see you.

But, May, they must have seen me coming and going many times.

Yes, my Jack, but that was in the dark, with the raining. That's okay. But is not okay in the light.

Nothing makes any sense in this country. They know

I come here, they see me arrive, but because it is dark and raining that's fine? If they see me leave in the light that's bad? My head hurts. I remember the fire-extinguisher and my head hurts more.

26

Jenson looks at me, out his window, back at me, then out his window again and, finally, back at me. While he looks around I smell myself. I stink. His nose is larger than I remember. The blood-red veins look ready to burst.

We had high hopes for you, Muir, he says. What a disappointment.

Sorry, Mr Jenson, but I don't think I'm cut out for a banking career.

You certainly are not, Muir, and that's why we are asking you to leave.

Are you firing me?

I think that's the term they use. I've never had to do it in my three years in the islands.

There's always a first, Jenson.

Mr Jenson looks at me with a hard sharp look that months ago might have had me worried, but now I don't care, not at all, not about Jenson or his fucking bank or any of the white-shirted pricks who work in it. They can all go and get fucked.

You're a disappointment, Muir, and if you were any younger I'd write to your parents and let them know how much of a disappointment. Look at you. You haven't washed since yesterday, no doubt. You stink and your work stinks. You're a disgrace.

I want to punch Jenson in his fat face, bust his bulging bloody nose. He is a racist prick, but he is right, I am a disgrace.

You're right, Mr Jenson. I'm sorry.

Get out, Muir.

A large part of me wants to burst into tears, fall on the floor and beg for forgiveness, but another, more manly part, is very clear that, simply, I am finished, done, dusted. I find a smile, bring it to my face and leave Jenson's office with a tall stride, walk to my desk and Beast, kick her, pick up my favourite pencil, grab my pocketknife, walk to Higgs, the ledger examiner, smile and say: Higgs, you're in charge now. Higgs looks up, then down, like he knows what was going to happen in Jenson's office before I entered.

You knew, right? That Jenson was going to fire me?

He busies himself with a stack of paper.

You suck, Higgs, you fucking suck.

I walk back to Franky.

I'm sorry, mate. I'm a fucking prick. Let me clean your room.

No need, Jack. Tarbo already has.

You've been a good mate, Frank. Thanks.

Things haven't turned out, Jack. You'll be right, once you find out what it is you want to do.

I don't think there's a living in what I want to do.

And that's that. My banking career over. Almost. The final details are worked out with Watkins. I want to go now, get out, through the front door, walk out with the Beast on fire behind me, but Watkins makes it clear that if I want a superannuation payout, and holiday pay, I better give a standard notice.

I thought you sacked me, I say.

We have, but we are giving you a chance, Muir, says Watkins, one you don't deserve. And, besides, we can't get another machinist up here for three weeks.

So that's it, they need me. They call for a replacement from the capital and when he arrives I work with him, another Tasmanian, for two weeks, and Jenson says I can stay in the mess for another fortnight until I get sorted. I thank him. I tell him it's very generous. I mean it.

.....

Work is better than it has ever been because there is so little of it for me to do. I help the Tasmanian as best I can. I show him where to sit, how to hold forms, statements, using most of the fingers and a thumb. When I show him how to get out of the chair and walk to the enquiry counter, he realises my mind is no longer in the building, but somewhere else. The Colonial Bank of Australia no longer has any hold over me. Did it ever? It was a job I had to take because Dad made me take it.

What's the smell? asks the Tasmanian.

It's her fluids, I say. You'll get used to it. Franky loves it. He takes a small bottle of it home with him every night and rubs all over his naked body before he goes to sleep.

Fuck off, Muir, says Franky.

When work is over I wait for dark and walk over to May's. Then I walk down to the Moroki Club and get pissed. I have no idea how I get back to the bank mess. I begin to enjoy the smell of my body. My skin has a new texture, somehow silky and smooth. I don't always shower in the morning.

.....

On my last day I walk up to Watkins.

Watkins, I say.

He looks at me.

Yes, Muir.

I'm sorry about coming around to your house with the truck.

He's not sure about the apology, I can see it in his face, and he's right, there's more to come.

But I'm not sorry about calling you a racist, I say, because you are.

His head goes back into his paperwork. I stand and look at the top of his head. There's a bit on the crown that is losing hair. He looks up.

Is that all? Muir.

No. You might want to think about a hair restorer.

His face runs a bright red. I almost feel sorry for him. I shake my head and walk out of the bank. Revenge is not sweet, it's nasty, but I don't seem able to stop wanting it.

27

Nothing to do now. Nowhere to go. All done. I sit around and drink beer. What a life. I spend a couple of days wandering around town asking if anyone has work for an ex–bank johnny, but no one seems interested, except for Wally Partridge, the bloke who runs the local electrical shop. Partridge is a fat prick with a beer gut, slimy, smooth skin and oiled hair. He looks out from behind his desk and says: Can you do books?

I worked in the bank, Wally, I say. That's all I did, books. Books is all I can do.

Can you sell shit?

Back home my dad had a shop full of shit and I worked in it most holidays.

Right. I'll let you know. Got nothing right now but someone might leave. Or die.

Maybe I could help them on their way.

Partridge looks like he wants to laugh but can't find the right muscles.

If you could replace a coon I'd shoot one now, he says.

I don't laugh. There is no laugh in me. Partridge is just another racist pig and I have a sudden urge to split his nose and spill his guts. But, I think, I might need a job and he might be the only bloke in town who can give me one. Almost as soon as I leave his filthy office I realise I could never work for him and I could not face May if I did and I need to face May. Sweet, gentle, kind, loving May is my lifeline.

28

For more than a week I have been looking for a job and a place to stay, drinking in the Moroki Club and sleeping in. I've had enough. Except for this book, *The Fountainhead*, by Ayn Rand. It's all about this architect bloke who is a genius but no one can see it but him. The entire world of architects is against him and they do everything they can to destroy him, but he keeps climbing up his own ladder and falling off until he meets this strong-willed woman, sort of falls for her, then rapes her. I hate him for that. She goes off and marries two other blokes but never gets over him and eventually they become lovers and marry. I don't get that bit. How can you marry someone who has raped you? But the architect, Howard Roark, inspires me with his tenacity and his achievements even though he is a mad crazy bastard and sometimes an absolute fucking shit to people around him.

The book reminds me how much I love reading. I wonder who I can talk to about it. Margaret Baker? Of course. Yes. But no. Not possible. My guts remember the punch. And my own filth. It also reminds me that all my favourite fictional characters are outsiders, blokes who fight against the odds, who work alone and are often beaten up. Paul Newman is my favourite actor and *Cool Hand Luke* one of my favourite movies. Then there's Dustin Hoffman in *The Graduate*. He gets to have an affair with an older woman. That was never going to happen with me, not in the highlands, even given the number of ugly marriages among expatriates. Most of the white women up here are ugly too. Not physically, but psychologically, and, as far as I can tell, most of them are racists. My favourite female actor, oh yes, Julie Christie. In *Doctor Zhivago* she's an outsider and both a whore and a Madonna and she shoots some nasty bastard who has raped her, tormented her, used her and can't leave her alone. One night I dream I'm in *Doctor Zhivago*, I save Julie from the rapist and then she wants me. I wake up wet and sticky.

.....

My papers keep arriving. They stack up in the corner of my room. I don't read them as they arrive anymore and some I don't read for weeks and then I read them all at once and out of order and I lose track of time. Too busy fucking and getting pissed. When I finally open them I call, again, for Jesus because most of the news is bad and mean. All that early, heavy, intense Christianity has left me, except when things go wrong, or go bad, or surprise the bejesus out of me, because then I call for Him. Calling his name helps, just then, for that instant, even though nothing changes and there is no ongoing comfort.

The world has gone fucking mad, Jesus. The USSR has invaded Czechoslovakia. I can't believe it. The Czechs are led by a good bloke called Dubček who lets kids wear their hair long and play The Beatles, and the Russians are led by a murdering communist bastard called Brezhnev who is the ugliest looking communist in the history of communism. Brezhnev has kidnapped Dubček, taken him to Moscow and is pretending they are having a nice time together drinking cups of tea, reading books and watching their favourite television shows. What's going to happen? Will there be another world war? Will East Germany invade West Germany? There's more amazing news, Ringo Starr has quit The Beatles. Jesus! Oh, no, there's been an earthquake in Meckering. Forty seconds it lasted, 6.9 on the Richter scale and it destroyed the town. I was there once, with my aunty and uncle, on a trip to Kalgoorlie. I didn't meet anyone. We just stopped to get petrol and Uncle Clem bought me an ice-cream. There are often tremors up here in the highlands. I quite like them, reminds me I'm not the only one unstable. And the students are rioting like mad in Chicago, New York, Paris, Amsterdam, London, even Sydney, everywhere but Perth. And Moroki – because in Moroki we have all the free love we can handle.

And I catch up with all the news from the Mexico Olympics. I love the Olympics. We get some news on Radio Australia but I don't get the full reports until I wade through the stack of papers.

The great highlights are the Bob Beamon massive long jump, the Dick Fosbury amazing high jump and, of course, local Perth girl Lyn McClements winning the one hundred metres butterfly. Not only is she good-looking, she is tall, strong and athletic. And white. But the real highlight is the black power salute by the two American sprinters when they stand on the dais to get their medals for the one hundred metres sprint. The other man with them, the silver medallist, is a white man, and an Australian, Peter Norman. I read the story again, look at the photograph again, and I imagine myself standing up there with them, arm raised high.

．．．．．

There's a knock on my door.

Come in, I say.

It's Franky.

Did you hear about Haines? he asks.

No.

He smacked Tarbo in the head with a table tennis bat.

What? What for?

For burning the pork chops.

Did you call the cops?

Of course. Anyway, Tarbo's gone. Taken his wife with him. You reckon you could ask one of your coffee buying mates if they could help us out with a new houseboy?

Sure.

......

There is a knock on the door. I am almost awake, but not quite and still half pissed from last night at the Moroki Club. I open the door and there's Tom Exeter. Nice bloke. Good chap. Works for the Byrne boys. Lives with Felicity, The Legs.

Jacky, he says. You awake?

No, mate, I'm asleep and I'm dreaming of you. Any minute now I'm going to spoof in my sheets.

He shakes his head.

Listen, he says, I've found a new houseboy for you. He can start tomorrow. He heard what happened to Tarbo and he said he'll work for the bank but not for Haines. It just means Haines can't do his turn with the menu.

Some blokes will be pleased about that. Thanks, I'll tell Franky.

Jack, you want to go on a trip up into Kia country? I'm off for about three days. You haven't been up there yet, have you?

You leaving Felicity? You mad?

He laughs.

Hang on, if you're leaving Felicity, I'm staying.

Flick has gone home to the UK for three weeks. We're both safe.

I haven't been into Kia country. I've heard about it, about the people, their aggression, readiness to fight and their ingenuity. Maybe a trip with a sensible man is just what I need to clear my head.

You serious about this? I say.

You ever seen a face like this talk bullshit?

Okay, I'm on board.

Exeter's a good bloke. Maybe they're all good blokes. Maybe it's just me, my secret moral code, my inability to concentrate, to think clearly, to make a go of opportunities and the rush of hot blood to my head at a time of tension and my inability to restrain myself when it comes to sex, or drink. I look at Exeter. I can see a fun drive up ahead, lots of tall stories, lots of dangerous situations, a few beers and I'll be away from the nothingness that shrouds my days. Not just nothingness, but uselessness, and the misty clouds in my head that thicken when Dad's voice enters: Pull your socks up and get on with it. Something. Anything. Or you'll be useless all your life.

Give me thirty seconds to grab a toothbrush, I say, maybe a change of undies and a couple of condoms. Oh, and I'd better give Franky the good news about the houseboy.

Exeter laughs as I scurry away. In no time at all we are in his Land Rover and heading out of town, away from the bank and the pressure to make a decision. To stay or not to stay? If you are an expatriate without a job the administration gives you about a month to find one or you have to head home. A few days up in Kia country will give me time to think about my future.

29

Exeter drives carefully, not like Huxley or Merkel. He is a man who wants to live into old age without battle scars. At first I recognise the terrain, the coffee plantations, the trees, the shrubs, not that I know their names, but I have seen them all before. Then he points the Land Rover up, its nose sniffing the higher ground, checking the safety of places it has not been before. The native line alongside the road thins and the vegetation thickens. Every so often we stop at a trading store and Exeter gets out to chat with the local trader. I wander about, not too far from the Rover, checking out the scenery, what little I can see through the trees. Not too far. Don't want to get lost in the jungle. Never know what might be in there. Shut up, Jack. There's nothing in there. I shake my head.

When we get to Kia country Exeter has a lot of businesses to visit, people to talk to. We have a room each in the local hotel motel. When Exeter has to drive out of town, into the bush, he takes me with him. The bush is different up here. Thicker. Greener. Impenetrable. If anything got in there it would never get out. But there is something trying. No there isn't. There's nothing. My head shakes.

The locals are shorter, and their bodies like stacks of walnuts. The women are forever carrying things hanging off their heads. They don't look at me, or if they do, they seem suspicious. The air is cooler. The girls show less flesh.

After lunch I go back to my room and read.

There's a knock on my door. I open it and Mike Hogarth walks in.

What are you doing here? I ask.

What do you mean me? he says. I should ask you? I'm a bloody patrol officer and this is my district. I could have you arrested and shot.

What for?

Anything, he says. But first, you want to come out for a drive? Somewhere dangerous. Right out there in the thick of it all where men are men and the women are even tougher.

All right, I say. As long as you do all the talking.

He does, I barely get a word in. As soon as we climb into his Land Cruiser, it and his mouth get into gear, but his mouth doesn't stop when the stick hits neutral. Yes, Hogarth did go to Timbertop with Prince Charles and his family was shocked when he decided to become a patrol officer on a far-flung piece of empire.

Hardly a bloody empire, he says. And we only took these islands on because no one else would. But that's what my mother insisted on calling it. She thought I was heading off to uni to do law.

Mine too, I say. She was convinced I was lawyer material. My older brother is. What's articles? He's doing them.

That's what they call what you have to do before you become fully qualified. It's like your probation period.

Why don't they just call him a cadet lawyer?

Not done, old chap. And neither is Margaret Baker. I hear you had a bit of bother.

Hogarth is driving along a dirt road. All the roads are dirt but this one is different, the vegetation closer to the edge, less room for those on foot. The trees are taller and the understorey heavier. There are no bears in there, or tigers, I know that, or no evil demons, but there are people in there somewhere, people who are not like those in Moroki.

Has there been trouble out this way? I ask.

No, he says, not especially, just the usual. Some bloke from one tribe speared another bloke and now there is a full-scale war on. You didn't answer the question.

I wasn't sure it was one.

Okay, I'll make it one. Have you got the hots for Margaret Baker and has it led to anyone punching the shit out of your face?

No, not that far yet. Shit, Mike, she likes me. What would have happened if Prince Charles had fallen in love with a girl he met down at the deli on a Saturday morning? His mum would have brought him home, right, and everything would have been hushed up.

He did.

What?

Well, he got it off with a girl he wasn't related to.

Anyway, it doesn't matter. I haven't got a job. I've got no prospects. I'll have to leave. I was fine until I got up here, Mike. I had a good start in life. My family are important people in my town and they sent me to the best, well, not as good as Timbertop, but the best we have.

What about May?

Fuck!

Yeah, I know. She'll make someone a great wife some day. And probably a white fella.

The forest is so thick I can't see past the front line of trees. From my window there is no sky and I can't see the clouds, but I can feel their heaviness. I have no idea where Hogarth takes me, what he does when he gets there, or why he is there.

30

Hogarth leaves me at the motel. I thank him. I find the lounge bar and order a drink. The waitress who comes out to serve me is a very attractive young girl who smiles with ease, takes my order with ease and has me assume that the next step will also take place with ease.

After my fifth beer I ask: What time you finish?

She smiles again but says nothing. Not long after, she walks out, takes my empty glass and says: What your number?

Seventeen, I say.

She looks pleased. Seventeen is around the back. As I get up to leave I can feel the lizard rising. In no time at all she is in my room, I am on top of her, and we are at it like two undomesticated brutes. Well I am, she lies there, submissive, as though this is all part of the motel room service. Maybe it is. When I am done and roll off she gathers herself quickly and stands beside the bed, looking down at me.

You a angry man, she says.

Angry? No, me not angry.

No hangry, hungry, she says.

You mean hungry?

Yes.

She stands looking at me and then I realise something else, she wants to be paid. I take out five dollars and hand it to her.

Thank you, masta, she says.

No, not masta. Jack.

She giggles and leaves the room. When she has gone I find my underpants and notice a yellow stain on the sheets. Strange, I think, not seen that before. I leave my clothes off and walk into the shower where I wash myself with vigour, once, twice, then again and once more the

172

lizard just in case the waitress has left me something I didn't order. My mouth stays open and I swallow large quantities of water hoping for an early piss and that the urine flow will clean my tube. Once clean and dry I piss and feel clean and allow myself to lie on the bed and doze. This country is crazy. I'm out in the sticks, I look at a woman, she looks at me, we want to fuck, we fuck. No bullshit, no flirting, no mucking around, straight to the point, in goes the lizard. I live in a country with free love and no one has to riot for it, it just is. Well, not always free, it just cost me five dollars.

I'm in the jungle. Alone. The tall trees are leaning into me, the bushes, the shrubs, the palms are moving in, closing, surrounding, crushing. Now I'm in the belly of a huge beast. The vegetation is slapping at me. I hear water running. It's getting ready to digest me. Footsteps. I flap my arms. The only way out of this is to fly. I can't fly. I run, but I don't move. Why can't I fly? I always fly. The footfalls are louder and closer. I scream. I flap my arms. I begin to fall. No, I'm not falling, the ground is sinking, the trees are falling. The beast is swallowing. I must wake up. Have to wake up. My feet are running but I'm not moving. I can hear them pummelling the belly of the beast.

I wake up. There's someone knocking on the door. Hogarth?

Jacko, yells Exeter. You ready for dinner. Got someone I want you to meet.

I'm sweating. My eyes are full of dust.

Right, I say. Who?

Just wait and see.

I splash water on my face then walk to the dining room hoping the waitress, whose name I missed, or forgot to ask, will not be there. Exeter is sitting at a table with an impressive-looking young man. They both stand.

This is George Kanluna, says Exeter, the first prime minister of this country. And, George, this is Jack Muir, the first head of your central bank.

We both laugh. I take a good look at the often mentioned George Kanluna. We put out our hands at the same time. His is soft but firm and I can see stringy, protruding muscles running up his arm.

Tom is good with the jokes, says Kanluna, but he may well be right. One day. For me. For you, I cannot know.

He speaks well, with a quaint way of putting words in a sentence. Not old-fashioned, nothing like pidgin-speak, but in an educated style all his own.

Yeah, I say. One thing you can bank on is that I'll never be the head of any bank.

We all laugh and sit down.

George is somewhat overactive politically, says Exeter. He heads a group of radical, university educated locals.

I look at his face. It is very black and handsome and I guess he probably has a white girlfriend.

The time has come, says Kanluna, for the people of these islands to run their own affairs. The islands belong to us and we are grateful for the work of the Australian expatriates, the Australian Government, even the bank johnnies, but this new parliament we have, with its appointed representatives, is no more than a token to appease our longings for a rule that must be by us, for us.

You see what I mean? says Exeter.

Just then the waitress walks by and smirks at me in a knowing way and I look at Kanluna and I can see that he has seen and I know he can also see the blood rushing into my face and setting it on fire.

Excuse me, I say. Toilet.

I leave quickly, looking about for the door with the familiar markings. I am lost in the dining room and my embarrassment is growing and just as I decide to make a run for my room the waitress comes up to me and says: You like piss?

Yes, I say, I like piss. But not here. The room for pissing.

She giggles and points to a room with no markings but I can see that it leads somewhere safe. Inside I take my lizard in my hand and squeeze it and say: You fucking piece of shit. What are you doing to me? Why can't you just go on a trip and mind your own fucking business and keep yourself soft and fucking flat and fucking quiet. All those years I waited, patiently, to break my virginity and now I can't stop. Fuck anything. Except men. No desire for men. Or a woman's back passage. I should have stayed home, bided my time, allowed things to develop at a more sedate rate and when she turned up, the one who loved me, married her and lived happily ever after.

When I get back to the table they have drinks. Kanluna looks at me and smiles. He knows all right. Does he hate me for it? I pile salt on my butter plate.

You know, this island was once a part of Australia, geologically speaking, he says. And that is why we share many species of flora and fauna. But geology has rendered us separate and separate we should be. I am not one of those who would see us swallowed whole by an Australian mainland state.

I told you he'd be interesting, says Exeter.

I had no idea, I say. We never did any of this in history.

You didn't do Australian history in history, says Kanluna.

We did some, I say. I remember Daisy Bates, Simpson

and his donkey, and the Kokoda Trail.

I am of the firm view, says Kanluna, like your Mr Whitlam, that Australia can never truly mature as a nation until it divests itself of its colonial appendages. By that I mean all these islands that surround it that it controls for a wide variety of reasons, not all of them benevolent. To be free, you must set free.

I wonder what it is that I have to set free. My parents? My anger? My salt dependence? I can see Kanluna marrying Margaret Baker and becoming island royalty. He reminds me of someone and I've been trying all through the meal to remember who and then it comes to me. It is my favourite actor of all time, Sidney Poitier. Just before I left Perth I saw Poitier in *To Sir with Love* and *In the Heat of the Night* and in both Poitier had courage and intelligence. I'd hated, loved, cried and stood my ground with Poitier. That was the me I took with me into the movies, but out here, in real life, I am a filthy lowlife piece of shit.

Are you all right, Jack? asks Kanluna.

I am holding a teaspoon full of salt in my mouth.

Oh, I say, the salt. I had a disease when I was a kid. The doctor told me to eat plenty of salt. Now I can't stop.

Exeter and Kanluna nod. I look at them. What are they doing together? One is black, handsome, strong, wears sandals, an educated man, a politician. The other is pale with neatly combed hair, showing the beginnings of a beer gut, wears shoes and long socks, an accountant. What do they have in common? Why are they friends? And why am I sitting with them? One knows enough about me to have the other one hate me. I can't figure it out. After dinner I go for a walk around the motel and hurry back to my room when the jungle thing plays havoc with my mind, the monster that wants to tear raw flesh from my living body. I know it's idiotic and I know that if there is no God then there's no devil, but I can't let it go. The head shaking doesn't seem to help.

.....

We are on our way back to Moroki, winding our way along an empty mountain road. Every so often there's a Byrne Brothers store. You know one is coming up because the on-foot traffic increases steadily and then explodes in the immediate vicinity of the store. Exeter is driving. I offer to drive but he says company policy would not allow it. Occasionally we see broken-down Land Cruisers on the side of the road.

There's a few of them, I say.

They'll all be gutted, says Exeter. The locals leave them there but take everything they can and use it. Eventually the whole thing will disappear and become part of something completely different. Or used in another vehicle.

Why did you want me to meet George Kanluna? I ask.

Exeter doesn't answer. He keeps his hands on the wheel.

Jack, did you fuck the waitress?

I can tell by the tone of his voice that he knows and that he doesn't approve.

What?

You heard me.

I don't ask the next question, the one about why he and Kanluna are friends.

31

Two papers arrive at the same time. I take them to my room and throw them on the stack of rolled papers. I've been stacking them again, in their rolls, unflattened, and later when I take one, the entire stack rolls off the dressing table onto the floor. I've been absorbed in my own shit again and neglecting the world's shit.

I unroll one. There are photographs of the new president of the US, Richard Nixon, who looks a lot like my old school headmaster, so I hate the man before I can give him a chance to prove himself. The Beatles have a new album out, another plane is hijacked to Cuba, and there's a story about Yale University's plan to enrol women students next year. I can see Margaret Baker as one of the first. She arrives surrounded by photographers and walks calmly up the main entrance, closely followed by her lover and constant companion. Me.

.....

Merkel drives into the driveway like the lunatic he is, tooting his horn, spinning his steering wheel, making great welts in the dirt.

You coming or what? he yells.

I am sitting on the veranda in front of my upstairs room.

What do you have in mind? I ask.

Get your shit and arse down here now.

I climb over the deck and slide down the post.

Merkel has the Land Cruiser moving before I have the door closed.

We'll have a few drinks in the Jungle, he says. Then? Who knows? Who cares. We'll fuck, wank, we'll go visit Jimmy Irish.

When we pull into the carpark, we pull up alongside George Kanluna as he gets out of his Volkswagen.

George.

Howard. Jack.

Kanluna knows Merkel? What is it with this country? Exeter and Kanluna makes some sense, but Kanluna and Merkel? We walk into the Jungle Bar together, find a space in the lounge bar and order three beers. Merkel and Kanluna chide each other about some party they once went to when Kanluna had to drive Merkel home because he ran his vehicle into a ditch and got bogged.

You still can't drive, says Kanluna.

Maybe not, but I always know where I'm going, says Merkel.

Down the other end of the bar three old blokes turn to look at us and one of them sneers. He looks like he thinks he owns the place. I sneer back at him. I have seen him before. He's an office clerk at Byrne Brothers, an alcoholic and one of those blokes you don't like as soon as you see him. What is he looking at? I don't ask. There are certain kinds of people you don't ask what they are looking at when you think you might know.

A couple of months ago I walked into his office because he had requested a bank statement in a hurry and our office boy was out on another delivery. He sneered at me then and he was sober, but he still stank of booze and smokes and I guessed he had a bottle stashed behind some files at the back of his office. Fuckhead is his name. Sorry, Farquahr.

You doing boys' work? asked Farquahr.

Just delivering something, I said. You got a problem with that?

No. Just don't make a habit of it.

Right then and there I wanted to punch the miserable shit's face, knock all his teeth out and bury him in a sea of shit. But I didn't. I turned and walked out.

As soon as the beers hit the bar Merkel orders three more.

Howard, says Kanluna, ease up, man. I have a meeting to attend later.

That may be so, George, but when you're out with men you gotta drink like men, says Merkel.

All three of us throw our heads back and laugh. As I bring mine down I can see Farquahr sneering again.

What the fuck is Fuckhead looking at? I say.

Him? says Merkel. He's a drunk piece of shit. Probably me.

We order three more and I say to the barman: And give one to the old prick down the end there.

What are you doing? says Merkel.

I'm making Fuckhead squirm, I say.

Good luck.

Kanluna picks up his glass and says: This is my last. I'm off to my meeting.

You don't have a meeting, says Merkel. It's that new woman you're with, isn't it? She's got you by the short and curlies.

Kanluna coughs into his beer.

This may be so, but it's better than living like you poor bastards.

Merkel yells down the bar: Three more up here please. We have an emergency.

Farquahr and his mates look up at us and the old man gets off his stool and yells: Why don't you fuck off, Merkel, and take your coon mates with you.

Silence. I can feel the heat rise inside me, overwhelm me. I turn to look at Kanluna. His black face has changed colour. It has a fiery, red tinge about it. He launches himself out of his chair and lunges towards the other end of the bar. Merkel and I are close behind him. We don't make it. A scrum appears in front of us and holds firm. Kanluna is yelling something in his first language. Merkel is yelling in a language I have never heard before and trying to climb over the top of the scrum. I try to crawl under it. A boot hits my cheek. The scrum collects us up and drags us out the back of the Jungle Bar. Behind us I can hear Fuckhead Farquahr calling out: And don't come back in here with your coon mates, you fucking gin jockey.

I break loose and run back in.

What kind of people are you? I yell. What kind of shithole is this?

The hotel manager, Jamison, grabs me from behind: Come on, Muir. Or they'll beat the shit out of you. Then he insists we sit at a table and that he buys us drinks.

We want to drink in there, says Merkel. We have a right and so does George.

Yes, of course you do, says Jamison, but Farquahr thinks he owns the place and today's his birthday. He's an old fool pissed. Can we cut him a bit of slack?

I'd like to cut the cunt's throat, says Merkel.

You all right, George? says Jamison. I'm sorry about what happened in there and when Farquahr has sobered up –

That's never, says Merkel.

I'll have a chat to him and tell him if he ever says anything like that again he's banned.

This sort of thing will not go on much longer, says Kanluna. Change is coming. Already we have a representation at government level and there are more changes coming, you know that, Jamison, I know that, Farquahr knows it too. That's why he hates me now. His time is almost over.

Kanluna looks sad and angry and ready to kill Farquahr. I want to kill Farquahr for him.

You can't go to a meeting like this, says Merkel. Stay and have a couple more until we all calm down.

Yes. I will. And I'm buying the next round and I will go into the bar to buy them and if Farquahr says anything I will kill him.

But he doesn't go, because Jamison brings a dozen stubbies out and puts them on the table.

Here you are, chaps. Hope this makes you feel better.

It doesn't. By the time we are down to the last couple Kanluna is talking bolshie, getting ready for the revolution, when his people will be running things and our people will be copping a beating.

That maggot better leave the islands before independence because if he doesn't I'll have him flogged, says Kanluna.

Merkel gets up and says he has to go to the toilet.

I look in my beer. It's a glorious day in the highlands. My nose takes in the multitude of smells. My head is hot. My arms are buzzing. My guts are fuming.

Jack, says Kanluna, I have seen you someplace before.

Yeah, I say, up in Kia country. We had dinner with Tom Exeter.

Yes, but before this. I am sure of it. Yes, I remember, it was Margaret Baker's birthday party.

Oh.

Kanluna doesn't warn me, doesn't hit me, doesn't tell me to fuck off and leave Margaret alone because she is only suitable for Hogarth because he went to Timbertop, or Prince Charles because he was there too and it would still be okay even if he did fuck a girl who worked in a deli because he is a prince and she's a princess. We sit in silence. I can feel the heat of Kanluna's body as I lean forward to take another beer.

George, I say.

Yes, says Kanluna.

You're not a communist are you?

No, but I do want independence for my country, that is what I want more than anything. If it means getting help from others, including communists, be that as it may. The tide is shifting and we cannot wait for the colonial authority. It was only last year that your Federal Government finally accepted Aboriginal people as full citizens.

You mean the referendum?

Yes, it was the final measure. They had been included as Australian citizens in 1949 when all of you changed from being British subjects to Australians but even then only the Aboriginal soldiers got the vote. The rest got the right to vote in 1962.

How come you know all this?

When you are fighting for your country's independence you make sure you know what you are up against. All this was a part of your shame I also did not know until I decided to get to know my enemy. You took their land, then they fought for you, died for you, and you did not recognise them as full citizens of their own land.

Kanluna says you, but I know he doesn't mean me. I hope he doesn't mean me. I took no part in the poll and I didn't take anybody's land. All I did was get born there. I wonder what Foley thinks of it all. I don't respond. I didn't know any of this. I didn't vote in the referendum because I'm still not twenty-one but I thought it covered everything and that it marked a great day in Australian history. My pink skin crinkles.

We sit back, drink. I wonder what Kanluna is thinking. I wonder if he is wondering what I am thinking. I want to tell him about me and Dorothy and May and Margaret and all the others and ask for his blessing, to know that when you leave out all the political talk that Kanluna is just like me, a man with needs, urges, desires. This means we fuck whoever allows us in, whatever their skin colour, their family background, school or religion. I want his approval. I want him to ease my shame.

The silence is broken by Merkel arriving back in a rush and yelling: Shit! We're outta here. George, your car's closest.

We run for Kanluna's car as the bar door opens and a dozen men stream out yelling: We'll get you Merkel, you gin-jockeying faggot.

We get to the car. We pile in.

Howard, says Kanluna.

Not now, George, yells Merkel. Just drive. I'll tell you when we're away. You'll be pleased. I promise.

Kanluna backs out too fast and hits the car behind. He doesn't stop. Men are still running for us and screaming. One breaks away. It must be his car. Kanluna turns out of town and drives until we come to a dirt track. He takes it. It's a bumpy, noisy ride and our laughter rises and falls with the bumps.

Stop, George, yells Merkel. I can't hear myself think and I gotta tell you what happened.

Kanluna stops.

I went to the toilet and Fuckhead was in there, so I kneed him in the back and he fell, banged his head and fell into the trough, right into his own piss.

George and I laugh at the image of the racist pig swimming in his piss, the piss of the bloke before him and the bloke before him and so on until he's swimming in the piss of the entire country, of every race and every creed.

Did he shit his pants, and chuck his guts? I say. Because that would have made a perfect bath for the white prick.

You know me, says Merkel. The first thing I did was think of his safety and that maybe he needed some water on his head to bring him around. The tap was too far away so I unzipped my daks and pissed on his head. That brought him out of his faint soon enough, but just then some bloke comes in. Barely enough time to put my dick away and give him a good old hip and shoulder in the chest.

That was a bad thing to do, Howie, says Kanluna, but thank you. After independence you'll be safe, I promise you, but pigs like Farquahr will pay a price for treating us like animals.

He's harmless, George. There's worse than him.

Maybe, but back there, in the Jungle, he had some support. Maybe all he does is shout out what the others are thinking. To them we are coons, always have been, always will be.

Then Kanluna, the strong man of the future, throws his head in his hands and sniffs. I think it's a sob, not a loud crying sob, but a small quiet sob. Merkel and I sit still. Water wells up in my eyes. Nothing appears in Merkel's. He looks out the window.

George, I say.

I'm okay. We'd better go home. I will drop you blokes off.

He drops Merkel off at his Land Cruiser, waits to make sure he gets away without a bar-load of angry whites kicking the shit out of him and then drives me back to the bank mess. You religious, George? I ask.

I am a Christian, he says. I go to church most Sundays.

Lutheran?

Yes. And you?

I used to be, not Lutheran, Anglican. I was big on Jesus.

He drives into the bank mess driveway and says: Why is it that not one of you bank johnnies have a car?

They won't lend us the money, I say. We're bad risks.

He laughs.

You know I got fired?

No. Are you looking for work?

No. I think I'll go home, I say. Then I take my life in my hands and ask the question I have to ask. Margaret Baker: you know her well?

Of course, he says.

She's a princess, George, I can see that. I wouldn't touch her. I just wondered, you know, if you know what she'll do with her life.

Margaret has done well in school and will study at a university somewhere, probably down south in Australia. She will study something useful for our country, maybe law. She will be an important woman.

Why is she so precious, George? What's so special about Margaret, that everyone, black, white, wants to protect her?

Jim Baker, her father, is a big man, for both black and white. He is the man who brought peace to the highlands, between the Ubadi and the Managan. He walked into the middle of a pitched battle and stood there with his arms raised until all the men on both sides threw down their spears, bows and arrows and machetes. He is a man of great courage. And when he was a district officer, his administration was often called on to mediate between rival parties, black on black, black on white and even white on white. When independence comes, we want Jim and Margaret Baker to stay and many believe that Margaret is blessed with the best of both worlds, the black and the white.

Kanluna and I shake hands. His are large, firm. They are the hands of a man who does not have to prove his strength. I get out of the Volkswagen and walk up the steps. Kanluna drives off.

Inside they have set up the table tennis table and Haines is playing Paterson.

Come on, Prem, beat the shit out of the prick, I say.

Look, it's the gin jockey come home, says Haines.

Something shifts in my guts. Seeing Haines, hearing Haines, changes everything. It wasn't Haines in the Jungle Bar, he was nowhere near, but I could see him there, yelling at my friend George Kanluna, smacking him in the head with a table tennis bat, kicking him in the guts while he was down, my friend George, the only man I know who knows Margaret Baker and has not warned me to keep my distance, the only man I know who talks about something other than the next fuck, or where to get pissed and the only man I know who is fighting for something, not a free fuck or the right to wear your shirt out or flowers in your hair, but his country's freedom.

Who you fuck today, Muir? Some fucking bush pig?

That's all I need. I push Haines. He laughs. I push him again. Harder.

You're pissed, he says. And now you want to fight? You're a gin-jockey joke, Muir.

You are a fucking racist pig, Haines.

Yeah, so? There's a reason, Muir. These people are rock apes. That must make you a rock-ape fucker.

No one speaks out against Haines. No one speaks at all. They stand, some are half-hearted laughing.

Come on, Jack, says Paterson. Leave Haines alone. You blokes were never going to like each other. Come on, have a game.

Fuck off, Paterson.

Paterson is trying to settle things down, to create a calm where there is a storm, but I haven't time for calm. I have come out of a storm and now I want revenge. Haines is in front of me. He is the bank's Farquahr.

Haines looks at me, sneers and says: You're a sad fuck, Muir. You're troppo, you're fucking gins, you've been fired, and you've got no job, and now you're pissed, you're trying to pick a fight when you couldn't fight your way out of a wet paper bag.

You'd know about wet paper bags, Haines, I yell. I'll bet your room is full of them because every night you wank into one.

Haines throws his table tennis bat. It strikes my eye socket and rips at the soft flesh against the bone. He turns and struts away.

Someone yells: Fuck, Haines. You could've taken his eye.

You're a gutless wonder, Haines, I yell. Come on then, you and me, outside, now, no bats, just fists.

Fuck off, Muir.

Jack, settle down, says Paterson.

Someone stands and moves towards me. I follow Haines down the corridor, up the stairs and stop when he stops outside his room. My face is hot, my brain is hot, my arms, hands, fingers, legs, feet, toes, dick, arse, everything, hot. I am shaking. I can kill this man, this thing. My cheekbone itches. My hand goes to it and comes away wet. I look at my fingers and see blood.

You cut me, you shit.

Get fucked, Muir.

In his eyes and those sneering lips I can see Hitler and Stalin and every Nazi racist bastard I ever read about, ever met, ever dreamt about. All of them, things. The heat has nowhere else to go but at the thing. I am all heat. The heat blows. I'm on him. I have the thing.

Then everything goes wrong.

32

He took me down with his arms around my neck, throwing his weight on top of me. There was a sound as my head hit the floor, followed by my brain screaming: Dive dive dive. I went with my brain, diving and felt it close down, turn out banks of lights, all lights but that little one up the back. There was nothing then, a kind of dead, then almost something, but not quite anything, then intense pain, physical, and emotional.

His breath on my face, his spittle drip drip dripping on my cheek, his arms around my neck cutting off my air supply and his legs wrapped hard and fast around my legs, as though to make sure no oxygen snuck in through my toes to make its way up my legs into my cardiovascular system and find its way to my lungs to give me the life that I had hardly started let alone nearly finished.

I am alone on the floor now. He's gone from me. Something runs down my cheek, spit, but not his, mine. I am dribbling the dribble of a pathetic little man who has lost his heroes, his friends. A man no one cares for as he lies dying on a floor up high in the highlands of some godforsaken land where white men rule over black women and both black and white men kill you if they don't like you or at the very least drop you like a sack of potatoes and stomp on your testicles as though they have fallen from the sack and are of no further use. Snot joins the spittle but before it reaches the floor a small stream diverts into my mouth where I taste its saltiness. I need salt, salt cures everything, suck that salt, more salt, nose, send more salt. Hang on, blood, fresh, and more blood than would seep from a cut made near an eye from a tossed table tennis bat. The nose on my face is bleeding. Is it broken, smashed into a messy potato salad of a nose as it hit the floor, throwing itself forward to cushion the rest of the face that followed?

My mother will not want to hear of my death. She will scream and yell and attack herself, blame herself, the mercury poisoning, my old school, my father, my older brother, anyone and everyone who ever lived. She wanted much for me, but never my death.

.....

I get up, stand still, find my feet, walk into the bathroom, splash water over my face and dry it with toilet paper. I look in the mirror. I don't recognise the face. There is heaviness and darkness and its lines are deeper. There's blood in the hair, seeping from a cut near one eye and oozing from the nose. Shit, there's someone there, no, no one, just the shadow of a boy I once knew. Yes there is. Someone behind me. I turn. William Foley.

You all right? he asks.

Yeah, I say. Nuh. I'm fucked, Foles.

Sorry I wasn't here. I was up the road. I would have stood by you.

You're always up the road. No wonder we didn't get you with the fire-extinguisher.

Foley laughs.

Seriously, you don't look good. You want me to take you to the hospital?

Nuh. Thanks. I'll be all right.

Your nose?

I don't think it's broken, just smashed.

You want me to kick the shit out the racist pig?

There's too many of them. Foles?

Yeah.

Then I tell him the thing I haven't told him because I resented him moving so quick on Dorothy and I wanted

190

to see if her racist father would send his men to beat up a black man.

Foles, I should have told you before. I'm a prick.

What are you talking about?

Dorothy's father is a policeman. Watch out for him. Some of his boys beat me up.

Shit. You serious?

Yeah, be careful.

Foley puts his hand on my shoulder. I want him to hold me. I want to smell his manliness. He takes his hand away. I leave him in the bathroom and step carefully down the stairs. The bank johnnies are still at the dining room tables, talking, some drinking coffee or beer. Their heads lift but they say nothing to me. I say nothing to them. Someone stands. I think it's Franky.

Jack, he says.

I don't look at him or them but I can feel their eyes scanning me.

Jack, says Franky.

I run out the door. I don't go far. Three houses down the road is a place owned by an expat who is hardly ever there. I lie down in his yard and cry myself to sleep.

I wake up when the rain starts. I cry a big sobbing jerking cry, get up, walk back to the bank mess, stand under Haines' room and throw a stone at his door. He comes out to the balcony and I say: Can I see you, please, Haines. Just for a minute. He walks inside. A minute later he is with me in the yard.

I'm sorry, Haines, I say, for attacking you. I still think you're a racist, but I had no right to attack you. I'm sorry. I don't know what's happening to me, Haines. I don't have a job. I have no idea what I'm doing here. My life is shit. I thought you were going to kill me on the floor. A part of me wishes you had. I know I wanted to kill you.

Haines says nothing. I have been looking down. I

look up. There are tears on his cheeks. Does he pity me? Is he crying because he nearly killed a man? Is he crying because he always cries when someone he knows is crying? Is he crying because he too can see the sad demented life we live here on these islands of free love and madness?

Sorry about the bat, says Haines. I've got a temper.

Then I see it: Haines is not the thing, the thing is not out there, in the jungle, it's in here, me, him, Merkel, in all of us and Haines is just another sad pitiful man like me. And a racist.

I put out my hand. He puts out his. We shake. He doesn't squeeze the life out of my hand, just holds it then lets it go. I turn and walk away, down the road, along the street. Hordes of highland people walk in both directions. Many of them carry fruit and vegetables I recognise but still don't know the names of. Some of them look at me. Most don't seem to notice me. A couple of maries laugh as I walk by. Do they know me? Have I been inside them? I think of my mother. It seems to me that I am more like her than I know. She is often up, then down. Are we schizophrenic? I have no idea what it is to be schizophrenic, but it seems we have something wrong with us, something more than a pink-skinned disease that means you can't concentrate and get hot and upset before your brain can step in and tell you to calm down, relax, that life doesn't have to be this way and that you don't have to get so angry about things you have no control over. I want to rest my head on her bosom and cry, tell her I love her, that I have messed up my life, that I am a filthy pig, that I am sorry, and ask her to help me and forgive me. I shake my head and flutter my hands. I can't believe what I'm thinking. What kind of bullshit is this? I'm a man. My father is a man. Men don't run home to their mothers and cry into their bosoms. They laugh as soon as a crying woman leaves a room. All that emotional nonsense, that's women's business. Not for men. Men are strong, straight, tall, firm and solid. One thing is sure, I want to go home. But first I go around to May's house and lie in her arms.

Jack.

Yes.

You fighting again?

What do you mean, again?

I know, Dorothy and her father's men. And the fight for George Kanluna.

How do you know all this?

In the highlands, words are quick. And I know you and Margaret Baker.

I have nothing to say. She knows everything.

May, I want you to promise me one thing. If Howard Merkel comes to your house, you won't let him in.

Why you have to say this?

Just promise me.

．．．．．

I get up to leave. May is sleeping. I don't wake her. In her sleep she reminds me of a painting. I have no idea where I saw it or who painted it, but the painting is of a sleeping black woman, a woman who was clearly at peace with her world and all you can see on her face is her beauty, no stress, anger or sadness, pure beauty. One finely shaped but strong arm lies across her chest.

I want to wake her and enter her one last time, but I don't. I lean down and kiss her forehead.

When I get back to the bank mess, Franky is sitting in the dining room.

Jesus, Jack, he says. You look like a truck ran into you.

I smile.

I'm sorry I didn't step in, he says. I thought it was best

to let the bulls charge each other. And you were spitting on everyone anyway.

That's all right, mate, I say.

What are you going to do?

I'm fucked if I know, Frank.

I'll come see you off.

To make sure I leave, you mean.

We laugh.

33

Merkel is waiting for me. It's my last night in the highlands.

Jacko, he says, I can't make the airport, but I thought we could have a couple of drinks up at Jimmy's. Hop in.

I don't want to, but I do. One final drink with the men who started my sexual revolution, one I didn't have to march for, occupy a building for, or go to jail for. And in the house where it all started.

Okay, I say. But I'm not staying long. I'm tired, Howie.

He doesn't answer.

Then he stops and turns on the cabin light.

What happened to your face? he says.

After George dropped me at the mess, I had a fight with Haines.

What's he look like?

Lot better than me.

Merkel laughs. He drives up to the Highlands Hotel, buys half a dozen bottles of Banda Beer and a bottle of rum.

I won't be drinking, Howie, I say. I think my Banda days are done.

He holds up the rum. I smile.

Inside the house there is only one light on, in the living room. We walk right in. Jimmy is sitting in a chair, slumped.

Jimmy, you all right, yells Merkel.

Jimmy looks up but there is no laughter in his eyes.

We have a problem, he says.

We? What kind of a fucking problem do we have, Jimmy? asks Merkel.

There's a girl in my bedroom.

Yeah. So?

She's dead.

Jesus Christ, Jimmy, did you fuck her to death?

Jimmy doesn't say anything. He sits. I feel like running. My knees shake. My guts move.

Who is she? asks Merkel.

I don't know, says Jimmy. I saw her across the street, called her over, she came inside and we went into the room. She even seemed to be enjoying herself, then she went limp.

How do you know she's dead?

She's not fucking breathing. She has no fucking pulse. Fuck me, Merkel.

What are you going to do? Jimmy, you're the fucking native welfare officer.

Jimmy jumps out of his chair and screams: I know what the fuck I am, you dumb cunt. Will you help me? Will you fucking help me? Will you? Help me, fuck you, help me!

Merkel stands very still. I run from the room, outside, into the bushes. My guts fall out my mouth. I lean over and drag everything up, out, and then I keep dragging, searching, for more, anything. My fingers are in my mouth, at the back of my throat. My guts jump. My back arches. All I get is air. Fingers go deeper. Dry as a salt lake. Nothing. The thing is everywhere. I lean against a tree. I hear voices. Merkel comes out, gets in his Land Cruiser and drives it towards the back door. Jimmy Irish opens it and Merkel backs hard against the opening. I don't look. It might be Mary, my first love. Jesus! I know what they will do. They will pick up the body, carry it to the door and put it in the back of Merkel's Cruiser, the limp dead body of a woman Jimmy Irish called into his house from across the street.

I stand a coward. The coward has no idea what they will do next. The coward does not want to know. He knows he has to get out of the highlands, the country, the almost nation full of love and hate and joy and madness.

Merkel and Jimmy Irish climb in the Land Cruiser. They don't look for the coward. They don't call out for him. This is their place. He no longer exists.

Merkel drives out of Jimmy's driveway. The coward follows and watches them into the darkness. He stands in the rain until he is soaked and shivering. He thinks about standing there forever. He moves slowly, so slowly he can feel every joint bend, shift, bend, shift. And he can hear every sound of every movement. The sounds multiply. He imagines he can hear every sound ever made, anywhere, anytime. His head is hot. His body shivers.

34

Exeter drives Franky, Foley and me to the Moroki airport. We wait in the lounge. The plane sits on the tarmac. I want to be in it, on the move, at the end of the runway, in the air, up, away, home, with The Beatles in my ear.

Merkel not coming? says Exeter.

He's busy, I say. We said goodbye yesterday.

We shake hands. I hold Foley's a little longer, wanting to wrap my arms around him. I turn away as I feel a sob rise. I turn back with a smile. They smile. I look back at them as I near the last door. No Kanluna. No Margaret. No May. I am leaving again but this time there is no final kiss. The three men wave through the glass as I walk across the tarmac. The hostess greets me at the top of the stairs. She's white. I don't smile. I have a window seat. I don't look out. I can see my brother Thomas at the other end, in Perth. He will pick me up and drive me to his flat. The next day I will catch the train to Bunbury where Mum and Dad will meet me. Mum will cry without knowing why. Dad will guess things and shake his head. I won't say much. When I get home I will walk in the bush behind the back paddock, among the jarrahs, marris and banksias. I might break a few branches and lie down on the shiny eucalyptus leaves.

I remember saying once that I'd have to be dead before I'd take a job in the family business, but that's what I'll do when I get home to Genoralup. It's time to let Dad have a crack at my life. He can't do any worse than me. I'll do anything he says, except join the Rotary club.

35

At Sydney Airport I don't pick up a paper. I move slowly from one gate to another, collecting my baggage as I go. Then I sit. I have no idea how long. Eventually I climb on board another plane.

......

I'm on a Qantas Boeing 707 over the Great Australian Bight. The air hostess brings me a meal. I know the names of all the vegetables. They have no taste. I keep asking her for salt because she smells like a highland morning after a solid rain, and she's blonde, leggy, beautiful, her breasts are a nice neat fit with the rest of her and I want to take her into the small room at the back of the plane and ask her if she'd like to fuck, then help her with her panties and drop my daks and stick the lizard into her and push and shove and go in and out until I'm ready to burst and then, when the bursting is done, ask her to remove all her clothes so I can look at her soft whiteness and remind myself even though I have never seen it before and hold her nakedness next to mine and try to love her but I don't and never will because she's a Madonna, and white, oh so white, and I am a whore.

Could I have some more salt, please? I ask.

You like salt? she says.

I have a craving, I say.

And because of the salt my mouth is dry and dusty and I drink lots of Tooheys New and because of the beer I get up every thirty minutes and go to the toilet. When I piss, the lizard itches and experiences a slight burning sensation. I wonder if it's the Australian beer.

I fall asleep. I am in George Kanluna's Volkswagen and there is a dead body on the back seat. He doesn't seem to know it's there and I can't tell him. I try to. I want to. But I can't. He stops the car and turns around, ever so slowly, as though he knows he will see something. I wake up in my room, shivering, sweating, and full of fear that he will see the body and know I put it there. Then I'm puzzled: he already knows it's there?

I wake up in the plane and get up for another piss. The plane is flying nice and steady. I walk towards the front, hoping to meet the hostess coming the other way and that we will touch as we turn sideways and pass between the seats and I will smell her loveliness and look closely at her delicate hands and want them to hold my lizard. Maybe one of the pilots will invite me into the cockpit. I've heard it happens and that the view of the world from a great height is something to remember.

I can go no further, there's a curtain, not quite filling the gap, and behind it I glimpse the hostess and a man in uniform, a pilot. There's movement. The curtain is pulled. Did I see her and the pilot kissing? I did. I am sure of it. The Madonna is not a Madonna. She's a whore. Or is she? Maybe she's engaged to the pilot. I return to my seat. The hostess walks down the aisle. I don't look at her. Now I remember who she looks like, Megan Stirling, the girl who kissed me goodbye at Perth Airport. Maybe I'll ask Megan out, make her laugh and she'll kiss me. A kiss would be nice. I miss a kiss.

My head falls forward. I lift it up, then it falls again and I dream I'm out with Megan Stirling. When we get back to her place we kiss. The lizard grows and keeps on growing. I try to contain it. It breaks through my pants. Megan doesn't seem to notice. I'm angry with the lizard. I have to get out of the dream. I wake up. The lizard is big in my pants, but I'm dry.

Fuck, Jimmy, a dead girl in your bedroom. I can't concentrate. I feel sick. I'm tired. My head is hot. Margaret

Baker looks at me, not really looks at me, because I'm on a plane, and she's in Sydney, but I know she's thinking we have no future, that I'm a coward. I write her a long love letter inside my head, knowing it will never see paper and that Margaret Baker will remain forever the princess of my dreams. Then there's May, gentle, kind, simple May, my Mary Magdalene. There I am again, a coward. I should have stayed behind and protected her. If Merkel knocks on her door, she's doomed. If he does I'll kill him. No. Did I do something about the dead girl? Did I say anything to anyone?

The coward slumps. He left his girlfriend, even though he knows she has no blood, no period, that she might be pregnant.

The coward has a window seat. He looks out as the plane crosses the final splash of water to fly over the vast emptiness, the flatness, the dryness, and heads up the land mass for Perth. He cries for his mother. He longs for his father.

The plane dips, drops from the upper world of blue into a shroud of white. He's come too far. It's too late to turn back. He thinks he can hear music.

The plane dips further, shudders, and moves into heavy cloud.

Acknowledgements

I would like to acknowledge that this book was conceived and written in Menang Country in the Great Southern of Western Australia.

The title of the work was deliberately chosen to echo a fine novel by Randolph Stow, who won the Miles Franklin Literary Award with *To the Islands* in 1958.

Surprisingly, there are always a lot of people to thank when you write a book on your own. There's my publisher and editor, Georgia Richter. Given the joys of working with Georgia I could just leave it there but I have to mention Clive Newman who kept encouraging me to write again. Then there are old friends: the man who put me back on track, Ken Spillman, the man who continues to offer sound and smart advice, Chris McLeod, and the woman who keeps me close, Grytsje Doust.

This book was not easy to write and two others helped beyond measure: Brian Malone and Piet Claassen, who not only read early drafts, they also informed the final work. Two others helped in particular ways: Harley Coyne and Andrew Wenzel; and Deborah Spittle again applied her sharp eyes. Readers of early drafts who offered encouraging words included Warren Flynn, Todd Shilkin and Louise Austen. And a final, deep acknowledgement for the fine proofreading of Naama Amram.

About the author

Jon Doust was born in Bridgetown, Western Australia, and spent his high school years at a private boys school in Perth. He failed his final year due to rebelliousness, drinking and surfing. After school his father insisted he take a job in a bank. The bank in its wisdom chose him for higher office on a South Pacific island. Out of that disaster came much good and Jon recovered well enough to attend a university and get a degree. He went on to write two children's books and a novel, *Boy on a Wire*, which was longlisted for the Miles Franklin Literary Award in 2010. *To the Highlands* is the second work of this trilogy, which is called One Boy's Journey to Man. Jon lives with his wife in Albany, Western Australia, where he writes in a smart house, runs, surfs, grows vegetables and agonises over the future of everything.

First published 2012 by
FREMANTLE PRESS
25 Quarry Street, Fremantle 6160
(PO Box 158, North Fremantle 6159)
Western Australia
www.fremantlepress.com.au

Consultant editor Georgia Richter
Cover design Ally Crimp
Cover image Amy Deskin, Old bed, Getty Images
Printing Everbest Printing Company, China

National Library of Australia Cataloguing-in-Publication entry

Doust, Jon.
To the highlands / Jon Doust.
1st ed.
ISBN 9781921888779 (pbk)
eISBN 9781921888922 (ebook)
A823.3

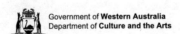

Government of **Western Australia**
Department of **Culture and the Arts**

lotterywest
supported

Australian Government

Australia Council
for the Arts

Publication of this title was assisted by the Commonwealth Government through the Australia Council, its arts funding and advisory body.